RACCOONS ON THE ROOF

"You know what?" Joel flung a final remark over his shoulder. "I think you'd better stop feeding those two raccoons, or else . . . !"

"Or else what?" Mandy ran after him, trying to catch hold of his arm.

He shrugged her off, his threat hanging unfinished in the air. "Just don't encourage them, that's all. It's not safe."

"What do you mean 'not safe'? How do you know? What's going on?" Mandy ran after him through the soft, warm sand. He knew more than he was saying, she was sure.

But Joel walked off without looking back, leaving her standing on the beach wondering what on earth his threat could mean.

Give someone you love a home!
Read about the animals of Animal Ark™

RACCOONS on the ROOF

Ben M. Baglio

Illustrations by Jenny Gregory

Cover illustration by
Mary Ann Lasher

AN
APPLE
PAPERBACK

SCHOLASTIC INC.
New York Toronto London Auckland Sydney
Mexico City New Delhi Hong Kong

Special thanks to Jenny Oldfield.
Thanks also to C. J. Hall, B.Vet.Med., M.R.C.V.S., for reviewing
the veterinary information contained in this book.

ISBN 0-439-23020-9

Text copyright © 1998 by Working Partners Limited.
Created by Working Partners Limited, London W6 0QT.
Original series created by Ben M. Baglio.
Illustrations copyright © 1998 by Jenny Gregory.

12

4 5 6/0

Printed in the U.S.A.
First Scholastic printing, May 2001

40

One

"Your turn, Mandy!" Joel Logan yelled.

The canoe they were paddling shot toward a cabin cruiser anchored close to the shore.

"No, me, me!"

"Okay!" Mandy lifted her oar out of the water.

Joel paddled hard through the clear blue waters. They missed the big white boat by inches.

The canoe veered to the left across the bay. "We made it!"

"Watch that sailboat!" Joel's grandfather, Jerry Logan, called. He and Mandy's grandpa, Tom Hope, were paddling their own canoe in front in a perfectly straight line.

1

"My turn!" Mandy called. She sat in the front of the boat, trying to get the hang of steering a canoe in the direction they wanted it to go.

They were aiming for Pine Island, across the calm waters off Blue Bayous. It was harder than it looked. "No, yours!" she called to Joel, who sat in the back. Their boat zigzagged hopelessly between small yachts and the bigger cruisers.

"We're going all over the place!" Joel moaned, paddling his oar so hard that the canoe rocked sideways.

"Yeah! It's fun, isn't it?" Mandy laughed.

Blue Bayous Island, shaped like a thin crescent moon, sat off the west coast of southern Florida. It was a seven-mile-long tropical island of palm trees, mangroves, and saw grass that snaked beneath the surface of the streams: *Pah-Hay-Okee*, or Rivers of Grass, as the Native Americans called this part of the world.

And Mandy could see why as they paddled crazily toward the shimmering, tree-fringed island, for the golden grass washed around the flimsy hull of their canoe in clear water only a few inches deep. "At least if we fall out, we won't drown!" she laughed.

"Yeah, but watch out for those 'gators!" Jerry Logan reminded her.

Three-yard-long alligators were supposed to lurk on the muddy banks, between the mangrove roots. But

Mandy had been staying with her grandparents at the Logans' place for two days now, and not a single "'gator" had crossed their path. "I wish!" she joked. There was nothing she would like better than to come face-to-face with a real live American alligator.

She and Joel paddled on, trying to work out a method of steering that didn't involve yelling at each other at the tops of their voices. They followed their grandfathers across the harbor toward a narrow inlet between the overhanging mangrove trees.

Though it was early morning and the dawn light was still pink in the east, the scene was alive with wildlife. Long-legged birds waded through the shallows, dipping their spoon-shaped bills into the water. Brown pelicans with massive heads and big feet spread their ragged wings and took flight, while in the treetops on Pine Island, noisy crows sat and cawed.

"To your left!" Jerry called, looking back over his shoulder. Though he was over seventy, his eyesight was as keen as ever. "Dolphin!"

They swung around, rocking the canoe. "Where?" Joel screwed up his eyes and squinted into the sun.

"Out to sea, beyond the mainland."

Mandy scanned the rippling surface of the almost tideless water. This was part of the Gulf of Mexico, fishing ground for dolphins and the weird, blubbery manatees, or sea cows, that cruised like submarines in and out of the bays.

"There! Can you see it?" Grandpa Hope picked up the binoculars hanging around his neck to take a closer look. "It just dived down. . . . No, there it is. It's back!"

And at last Mandy saw the dolphin. It rose out of the sea with its domed, blue-gray head and pointed nose, lifting itself clear and twisting as it leaped, then splashed back into the water in one flowing movement. The sea foamed and sparkled. Then the dolphin rose again, rolling in the water and disappearing with a flick of its tail.

"That's incredible!" she breathed. It was so big and powerful, yet playful, too. It seemed to frolic in the water for the sheer fun of it.

"He came to say hi." Jerry Logan took the dolphin's antics for granted. "They feed mostly at dawn and dusk, like a lot of animals here." Holding his paddle clear of the water, he waited until they'd decided that they'd seen enough.

Mandy kept her gaze fixed on the spot where the dolphin had last been seen. "Please come back!" she whispered.

"I guess he heard you." Joel pointed nearer still to land, where the dolphin had shown up once more, dipping down, then rising lazily this time. No acrobatics; just a slow, graceful trawl through the waves.

"What's he doing so close to the shore?" Mandy asked Jerry, who had lived in Blue Bayous for most of his life.

"Hoping for scraps from the boats," Jerry replied. He was all set to paddle the last stretch toward the inlet, still lean and fit, dressed in a dark blue baseball cap and checked shirt with the sleeves rolled back. He wore silver-rimmed glasses, and his face and arms were tanned from a lifetime of working in the sun.

For a short time, however, Jerry had lived in England. These were the years he spent in Yorkshire as a young soldier, fifty years earlier. That was when he met and married Mandy's grandma's friend, then called Barbara Eden. He'd brought her back here to Florida and they'd made a life together: he as a landscape gardener, she as a secretary, then as a mother and housewife. For all these years Dorothy Hope, Mandy's grandma, had written and kept in touch with "Bee" Logan.

When Mandy had first been invited to come with her grandparents to Florida, leaving her parents behind in Yorkshire to carry on with their vets' practice at Animal Ark, she'd heard the Logans' story. In her mind it was wonderfully romantic.

Grandma's friend had been a GI bride and had traveled halfway across the world to be with her new husband. Meanwhile, Mandy's own grandma and grandpa had settled cozily in Welford, Yorkshire.

They'd lived in Lilac Cottage all their married lives, and brought up Mandy's dad, Adam, there. They'd seen him through veterinary school and had been delighted when he and his new wife, Emily, had set up their practice in the same village. Now they did all they could to help life run smoothly for their family, and Mandy loved having them nearby.

Yet there was something risky and adventurous in what Barbara Logan had done. Mandy admired the way she'd left one life behind and started anew.

And what a place to choose to live, she thought, the moment she saw it. Stepping off the plane into the heat, driving down the Interstate in Jerry Logan's battered pickup truck, crossing Two Mile Bridge from the mainland onto Blue Bayous Island, and arriving at last at Pelican's Roost, Mandy had marveled at the scenery.

Bee Logan had flung her arms around Mandy's grandma and cried. She'd introduced Mandy to her twelve-year-old grandson, Joel, who had flown down to stay with them for the summer from his home in New York.

And the vacation of a lifetime had begun.

Now Mandy gazed out to sea, hoping for another

glimpse of the dolphin. She rested her oar across her knees, feeling it drip onto her bare feet. The water lapped at the sides of the canoe, rocking it gently.

"Watch out, look where you're going! Land ahoy!" Grandpa Hope cried.

But it was too late. The yellow canoe crunched against a thick mangrove root, which was twisted and coiled like a blacksnake. Mandy and Joel shot forward off their seats, waved their arms madly in an effort to regain their balance, and fell out of the canoe.

"Ouch!" Mandy sat down hard in the shallow water. She saw a blue crab scuttle along the length of the root, out of sight. A little way off, a big, glossy black bird with a long, snakelike neck flew off out of the trees.

"What happened?" Joel staggered up out of the water and caught hold of the upturned boat. "How come you weren't watching where we were going?"

"How come *you* weren't?" Though he was the same age as her, Mandy had already noticed a tendency in the Logans' grandson to blame her when things went wrong. He was a smart city kid who gave off an air of being bored by the things Mandy loved, namely animals.

"You were in the front!"

"So?" She groped underwater for her paddle, nearly tripping over another hidden root.

"So, you were supposed to steer!" Joel tried to wring

out his dripping white T-shirt and climb back in. "Hold on to this canoe, will you?"

I hope you fall out again! Mandy said to herself, watching him tip the canoe sideways. She was still knee-deep in the warm water, trying to hold the canoe steady. In the end, having made a big thing of the accident, Joel managed to clamber back in. But then he pushed off from the shore, making her wade after him. "Hang on, wait for me!" she protested.

Joel narrowed his eyes and jutted out his chin. He was looking over Mandy's shoulder at something in the shadow of the mangroves. "'Gator ahead!" He stabbed his finger toward the bank.

Mandy's heart jumped into her mouth, and she grabbed for the canoe, plunging through the water after it. An alligator with two sets of razor-sharp teeth, jaws that could snap her in two! She dived for the boat.

But Joel's face creased into a grin as she hauled herself over the side and sat gasping in the bottom. "Just kidding," he said, flashing her an innocent smile. "Come on, we're way behind the others. Let's get out of here!"

Mandy discovered that the swamps of Pine Island were a maze of narrow streams running between the strange mangrove trees whose roots formed arches, or props, that seemed to stride out into the water. It was a shady, shimmery world of tunnels formed by branches that met overhead; they were on a secret journey along unmarked routes, well away from the bright sun's rays.

"Spooky!" Joel said, paddling steadily now. Their grandfathers had kept ahead, judging their direction by the angle of the sun.

"How far are we going?" Mandy listened to the rhythmic splash of the oars, gradually getting used to the dim light and jungle scenery. It was like nothing she'd ever seen before, like a scene straight out of an adventure film.

"Who knows?" In the back of the canoe, Joel kept up his annoying habit of telling her when to paddle. "You now! No, stop. It's my turn!" It didn't seem to help, and they kept veering from bank to bank, crashing into the roots and getting their hair tangled in low branches.

"How are you two getting along?" Joel's grandfather glanced back to check.

"Fine!" Mandy called through gritted teeth. She had just pushed free of the bank once more.

"Okay, we're coming up to the clearing. There's a kind of lake on the island, in the middle of the wilderness area, where you can see cormorants and anhingas. And watch out for the roseate spoonbills!" Jerry Logan was a bird-watching fan, and the technical names rolled off his tongue.

"Great!" Joel muttered under his breath. "What do *we* care?"

Mandy wondered if he really was as bored as he looked; his face was set in a frown, and he was refusing to glance in the direction his grandfather was pointing. Or was this tough act for her benefit?

They paddled out onto the open lake, feeling the sun on their shoulders, shifting their weight to ease the numbness of sitting paddling for too long in one position. Here, the water was as smooth as a mirror. In the distance, a group of white birds with long stiltlike legs stalked and raked their yellow beaks through the saw grass.

"Great egrets!" Jerry Logan called, excited as a child.

Grandpa Hope pointed his binoculars in their direction. "Amazing long neck," he murmured. "It's shaped like an S!" Like Joel's grandpa, he loved to observe nature, lapping up all the new sights that Florida had to offer.

Joel sighed and sulked in the back of the boat.

"What's the matter?" Mandy asked. To her, all this was new and exciting, but she was fed up with Joel. "Don't you like animals and birds?"

"Nope."

"Well, I do!" In fact, she was already making a list of the species she'd seen since she'd arrived on Blue Bayous: brown pelicans and blue crabs, herons, turtles the size of laundry baskets, and now a bottled-nosed dolphin. "I don't see how you can say you don't like animals."

"Easy," Joel argued. "I don't like them. They bore me."

"What!"

"They're boring. I don't see the fun. They don't talk, you can't do anything with them —"

"Animals *do* talk!" Mandy interrupted. "Dolphins have their own language. Just because we don't understand it doesn't mean they don't talk!" She frowned and treated Joel to what she regarded as a big dose of scorn. "I suppose *you* came to Florida to visit all the theme parks and nothing else!"

"Yep."

This was too much. "Look, I don't mind all the cartoon characters and things," she admitted. "Mickey Mouse and Bugs Bunny and all the rest — they're great in their own way. But" — she struggled to find the words — "give me the real thing any day!"

"Not me," he insisted.

"And I suppose you'd rather watch a video than go out at night and look for panthers!"

"There are no panthers on Blue Bayous. Ask Grandpa."

"Well, alligators, then."

"You don't see them at night."

". . . Well, raccoons, then!" He couldn't argue with that. Mandy had heard them the night before, scrambling around on the wooden roof at Pelican's Roost.

"You don't see them, either. It's too dark."

Mandy gave up and began to paddle across the lake. *I wish James was in this boat instead of Joel!* she thought. James Hunter was her best friend back home in Welford. He would have appreciated the spoonbills, just like all the animals and birds they'd rescued together. Being a vet's daughter, Mandy's life revolved around wild creatures and domesticated pets. She dug the paddle into the calm water and pushed hard.

"Make for the main stream at the top end of the lake!" Jerry Logan called, noticing their canoe sail past. "You see it? A couple of yards to the right of the observation tower."

Mandy saw a wooden platform on tall stilts, and beside it another of the overgrown channels through the mangroves. Her grandpa was happy watching birds or "twitching," as he called it, and Jerry Logan was in no hurry, either. "What's at the far end?" she called.

"The Gulf of Mexico. You can't miss it!"

"We'll wait for you when we get there." The adventure of being the lead canoe along the narrow route would make listening to Joel's moans more bearable.

"I mean, those guys who get to go to the theme parks are having fun." He wouldn't drop the subject. "You can buy whatever you want: candy, soda, burgers, fries . . ."

How could Joel compare junk food to the natural marvels all around them? Mandy wondered. She gazed up into the green leaves of the arching branches, forgetting to steer a straight course upstream.

"And the rides are great, too," he went on. "Water rides are the best. I've been on the biggest thrill slide in the world and spent a whole day on the Bumper Surfing Simulator!"

"Wow!" Mandy kidded. She enjoyed the water rides, too, but she wouldn't let on to Joel. She allowed the canoe to drift, watching the patterns of sunlight on leaves.

"Better than paddling some crummy canoe," he muttered. "Nothing happening, nothing to see. It's a drag."

Whack! They hit the bank. *Crunch!* The canoe wedged itself between two mangrove roots. Something stirred in the undergrowth nearby.

"What was that?" Mandy said nervously, looking around. With her paddle, she tried to push the canoe away from the bank, back into the stream. The roots held them fast.

There was a slithering and rustling through the bushes. A large creature sank its feet into the mud with a sucking, oozing noise.

"Quick, back off! I'm out of here!" Joel yelled, trying to dig his paddle into the muddy bed of the stream and lever the canoe backward.

"We're wedged in!" Mandy could see exactly how the boat was trapped. "Did you hear that noise?"

There was another slithering, sliding movement, the sounds of twigs snapping and mud oozing. Then the creature appeared.

"'Gator!" Joel cried. This time it was for real.

"I know, you don't need to tell me. I can see!"

The alligator squatted on the bank ten yards from where they were trapped. Its legs were spread-eagled; its long, scaly body poised to launch itself into the water. But it was its head that held Mandy transfixed. It had gaping nostrils at the end of a rounded, leathery nose, dark, lizardlike eyes, and a wide, smiling mouth. And its teeth were white and terrifying.

"What are we going to do?" Joel whispered, swallowing hard. The alligator had them in its sights. It turned and lumbered along the bank toward them. Then it stopped and opened its mighty jaws.

"Look at that!" Mandy widened her eyes fearfully at the sight of the enormous pointed teeth.

"It's coming after us! Push, Mandy, get us out of here!"

The alligator took another step, lifting its squat legs

with their cruel claws. Still it had Joel and Mandy in its blank gaze.

Mandy pushed at the roots of the tree, forcing them apart, trying to free the canoe. Beneath them the mud churned up and clouded the water.

"Get a move on!" Joel levered with his own paddle. At last, the boat floated free.

"Reverse!" Mandy yelled, working the oar in the opposite direction. They were afloat, but the danger wasn't over yet. The alligator lumbered along the bank, crushing undergrowth as it came. Then it changed its plan. It turned and tilted into the water after them.

"It's following us!" Joel cried. "Paddle faster, Mandy; come on!"

The water closed over the alligator's scaly back. It began to swim. Now all Mandy could see, as she frantically plunged the paddle into the stream, were two sinister eyes and a long snout gliding through the water, gaining on them with every second that passed.

Two

"It's okay, don't panic!" Mandy paddled with all her might. The alligator cruised slowly after their boat. "'Gators don't attack humans!"

"Says who?" They were still lurching backward downstream. The back of the three-yard-long, scaly creature emerged from the muddy water as it surged after them.

"I read it in a book — I think!" Mandy's arm arched. She was breathless with the effort of shoving the canoe free.

"Well, this one does." Joel managed to stop the canoe and face it in the right direction, but the alligator had swum even closer. It could almost nudge their bright yellow boat with its long snout.

"They only attack if someone's been feeding them. Then they can't tell the difference between us and the food!" Even she had to admit that the giant reptile didn't have the biggest brain in the world.

"I know that!" Joel paddled furiously, back toward the lake. The boat rocked and tipped dangerously.

One lash of that powerful tail, one snap of those terrifying jaws, Mandy thought, *and the books could be proved wrong. The alligator would smash their flimsy fiberglass canoe like an eggshell.* She watched over her shoulder as Joel raised his paddle in panic and turned to smack it down on the creature's head.

"Don't!" she yelled. It would be even more dangerous to make the alligator mad. "Just keep paddling!"

Joel paused. The alligator kept its cold eyes fixed on them, nosing through the water, evidently wondering whether to launch a full-scale attack. Meanwhile, Mandy knelt in the front of the boat, paddling for all she was worth.

At last, after what seemed like an age, the tunnel of trees opened up, the sun dazzled, and the lake reappeared. There were Mandy's grandpa and Jerry Logan, quietly watching the blue herons from their own boat;

there were the white egrets wading in the shallows of a warm, peaceful world.

"It's okay, he's turning back!" Joel called.

Mandy risked another glimpse over her shoulder. The alligator had reached the edge of the lake and swum in an arc, away from their canoe. Something else had caught his eye, or else he was satisfied that he'd given the humans a scare and sent them on their way. Soon, he was heading lazily back upstream, looking like nothing so much as an old log floating on the surface.

Slumping forward, Mandy heaved a sigh.

"I told you they didn't attack people, didn't I?" Joel said. He ignored Mandy's gasping protests. "Say, that was kind of like the movies!"

She groaned. "It's okay saying that now!" He hadn't thought so at the time, with the alligator nudging at their canoe, showing them its savage teeth.

"Wait till I tell everyone back at school!"

"Big hero." How had he gotten over his fright so fast? Her heart was still thumping, her arms limp with effort.

"Yeah. Did you see those claws? I'd say they could slash through the hull of that boat, no problem. What do you think he was, four yards long?"

"Three."

"No, three and a half at least. And his face was real

mean! Do you know what I bet? I bet he was one of those nuisance 'gators they warn you about. You know, the ones that get fed by stupid tourists who don't know the rules. So instead of being scared of us, they come after us!" Joel's eyes were bright with adventure.

Mandy sighed again, wishing that he would make up his mind. "Whatever. All I know is, I was pretty scared."

"Nah!" Joel was suddenly a swashbuckling movie hero in a wide-brimmed hat. He had nerves of steel. "It was nothing."

"What happened?" Jerry Logan and Mandy's grandpa had spotted them and came paddling quickly toward them. "Did you get lost?"

"Nope. 'Gator ahead," Joel replied with a casual shrug. "Four yards long and pretty mean."

Mandy smiled and shook her head, catching her grandpa's eye.

"Come on, what are we waiting for?" Joel urged. "There's gotta be hundreds of 'gators up that creek, and I want to get a close look at another one of those guys!"

Suddenly, Mandy noticed, Joel didn't think animals were boring after all.

They saw many alligator sunning spots on the overgrown banks and many shadows that could have been alive. They saw shapes in the water that looked like rough, scaly backs and blunt snouts, but turned out to be driftwood floating gently downstream. But they didn't see any more alligators on their route to the open sea, and Joel couldn't play the hero again, at least on this trip.

"It's a little too late in the day," Jerry Logan explained, laid back and easy, pointing out yet another flattened area of undergrowth where the alligators might choose to sun themselves. "Or a little too early, depending on which way you look at it."

"How come?" Mandy had gotten over her fright. And she was seeing Joel in a new, friendlier light. She decided to write a postcard to James; one with a picture of an alligator on the front under a sign saying DO NOT FEED!

"They come out at dawn, when there are more things for them to eat: fish and turtles, raccoons, stuff like that."

Grandpa Hope glanced up at the sun as they emerged from the last of the mangrove tunnels and faced the sea. It was well clear of the horizon in the east. "So we're too late to catch sight of them first thing. But what do they do for the rest of the day?" He seemed pleased with himself for being able to keep up with Jerry Logan's pace, bracing himself for the journey around the headland and back into Pine Island Sound, then across to Blue Bayous once more.

"They rest up," Jerry said. "Then, when the sun gets

real hot, they come out and do some sunbathing. Around two in the afternoon. That's when you see plenty of 'gators."

Joel frowned. "That's, like, hours from now!"

"Sure, but we can come back another time. You're here for a good few weeks." Jerry Logan pointed out their new direction. "Stick close to the shore and we might get lucky," he told them. "There's still a chance we could see them in the mangroves over there."

"Or dolphins." Mandy looked hopefully out to sea. After the shadows of the swampland, everything was bright, light, and fresh.

"Squirrels and deer," Jerry suggested. "There are tons of those little guys."

"Wait! What are they?" Mandy's grandpa stopped paddling and pointed to a narrow inlet where a stream met the sea. He picked up his binoculars and peered through them.

"Raccoons." Joel's grandfather paddled steadily on.

"Huh!" Joel kept on after him. Back to his sulky, couldn't-care-less mood. "Who wants to stop for raccoons?"

"I do!" Mandy could only just see them, but she thought they looked cute. This would be her first sight of the creatures with the famous black "bandit" masks and black-and-white ringed tails. "Let's get closer!"

"No, take these." Grandpa leaned across to lend her the binoculars. "Better not scare them off."

So she put them to her eyes and adjusted the lenses. There were five or six of various sizes, the biggest about four times the size of a squirrel. She could see the black band of fur across their gray-and-white faces, their neat little hands and squat haunches. They were all busy at the shoreline, dipping their front paws into the sea. "What are they doing?" she asked.

"Washing their food!" Jerry Logan laughed. "It looks weird, doesn't it?"

"Why do they do that?" Mandy was fascinated. They seemed to be holding shells, dipping them time and time again into the shallow water.

"Who knows? I don't think anyone's found that out yet."

"Who cares?" Joel muttered under his breath. Obviously, raccoons weren't adventurous enough for him.

"They're cute!" Mandy protested. "They look like old ladies doing their laundry!" After they'd finished with the water, they seemed to scoop the contents of the shells into their mouths.

"A lot of people around here wouldn't agree," Jerry Logan told them. "Raccoons have a pretty poor reputation, as a matter of fact."

Two of the raccoons then pounced on the same shell

and squabbled over it, scrabbling at the sand as they pushed and shoved.

"Folks think they're greedy and dirty. They can carry disease, so some people treat them as a serious nuisance. They don't like them near their houses. A lot of people try to get rid of them."

"But how can they do that? They're lovely!" Mandy protested. "Look how clever they are with their hands!" She wanted to get closer, but Joel was stubbornly paddling in the opposite direction.

"They're smart," Jerry Logan agreed.

"Maybe, but they're still pests," Joel argued. "Everyone knows that."

"Well, don't get your grandma going on that subject," his grandfather warned. "You know how she is with animals." He looked at his watch.

"Speaking of your grandma," he said, easy as ever, "I told her we'd be back in time for a snack. What do you say we head off for Pelican's Roost before the sun gets real hot, put our feet up, and talk about what you want to do with the rest of your vacation?"

The Logans lived in an old-style Florida house built of wood and standing on a frame of tall stilts. Pelican's Roost had been their home since they were married, so

Jerry had spent a lifetime growing hibiscus and lilies in the semitropical garden, while Bee had crammed the house with cane rocking chairs, seashell lamps, ornaments, and photographs, first of children, then of grandchildren. Mandy loved its coziness, mixed with the exotic flame-colored plants in the garden and the sparkling view over the Gulf of Mexico.

"Jerry loves his plants," Bee Logan told Mandy's grandma as the two women sat on the porch drinking coffee. They got along well together, even after all these years apart.

Jerry Logan and Grandpa Hope were strolling under the trail of purple bougainvillea that grew up a white latticework arch at the bottom of the garden. "So does Tom," Grandma Hope replied. "Only in Welford it has to be tomatoes and leeks, not melons and oranges." She rocked gently in her chair.

Mandy sat cross-legged on the porch, playing a game of solitaire. She bit deep into the best homemade chocolate-chip cookie she'd ever tasted. Meanwhile, Joel had disappeared inside the house to phone his friends in New York.

"Jerry calls this our Garden of Eden," Bee murmured. "He named it after me before I met him, see. Barbara Eden. He built up a native plant nursery around the back: sea grapes and special types of mangrove trees. He's against the palm trees that you see all around. They're not native to Blue Bayous. And, of course, he tries to persuade all his customers to grow native, too. He's a 'Green Earth' man through and through." Jerry's nursery was called "Green Earth Gardens."

The easy talk washed over Mandy. She'd almost finished her game. In the midday heat, the garden buzzed with insects. A beautiful red-and-black butterfly landed on the dazzling white paintwork of a nearby banister.

Bee kicked off her sandals and put her feet up on a stool. She was a small, neat woman with short, gray hair, and was dressed in practical shorts and a light cotton shirt. "Not everyone agrees with Jerry though." She began the story of their new next-door neighbors, who had just finished building their grand house, complete with swimming pool and three-car garage.

"The Miller family own Moonshadow, as they've decided to call it. They aren't into sea grapes and mangroves. They like order in their garden. They have a man come in to rake the lawn every day and turn on the sprinklers, even when they're away." She described their jet-set lifestyle, flying between Chicago and Florida.

"Who's that, our friends next door?" Jerry Logan had

finished his tour of the garden and led Grandpa Hope into the shade of the porch. He delved into the cookie jar. "The problem there is not so much the plants as the animals."

"How come?" Mandy finished her game and scooped the cards up. The mention of animals had brought her to life.

"Animals don't figure in the Millers' scheme of things," Jerry explained. "Which is a problem, because right next to our garden, between the Millers and us, is a run for turtles, sea otters, and the like."

"Any raccoons?" Mandy asked. She remembered the way they scrabbled along the porch and onto the roof.

"Sure. They pass by on the way to the beach, have for as long as I can recall."

Her eyes lit up. "What sort of a run?"

"A track through the bushes," said Jerry. "They like to keep well hidden mostly. And the way I plan my garden, I leave them plenty of cover. But not Robert Miller; not on your life. He gets his gardener to cut it all back."

"That's a pity," Grandpa Hope agreed.

"It's more than that, it's a crime," Mandy protested. "Imagine ruining the animals' habitat! They were here long before the Millers!"

"As you can see, Mandy's on your side." Dorothy Hope smiled and went on rocking. "Except where alligators are concerned." She'd listened to the morning's adventure, half worried, half amused.

"Even with 'gators," Mandy said now. "I think they have much more right to be here than we do. I wish we hadn't disturbed the one on Pine Island."

Jerry Logan chuckled. "I guess he'll survive the experience. Do you want me to show you this animal run?"

Mandy was on her feet and out in the garden before the sentence was out of his mouth. "Which way?"

"Over there." He grinned at the others and led her off the boundary of the garden.

Soon she was crouching under the broad, round leaves of a sea-grape bush, examining a worn track in the sandy soil. "What are these?" She pointed to a broad trail of scuffed footprints.

"Turtles. And these small, neat ones are otters. Here!" Jerry beckoned her to show her a set of perfect prints, bigger than the otters', with a set of sharp claws making imprints in the soft earth. "What do you think these are?"

"Raccoon?" Mandy guessed.

He nodded. "And these smaller ones belong to a baby raccoon. We have three or four families using the run right now."

"Do you keep count?" She was fascinated by the various signs of wildlife.

"We know pretty well. Some of the turtles have already stopped using the run, due to what's happening next door. And a couple of raccoon families have cut out this patch of ground. But we still get six or eight coming through."

"When? Mostly at night?" Mandy was eager to learn.

"Any time of the day or night."

"Joel said raccoons were nocturnal." She touched the prints with her fingertips, peering into the undergrowth for further clues.

"Mostly they are. But not in this part of Florida. We have kind of special raccoons; smaller than average, and leaner. These are tidal. They come out at low tide, night or day."

"To find shellfish?"

He nodded. "And turtle eggs. Not too many folks know about our raccoons. Mostly they don't care, either."

At that moment, Bee Logan called Jerry's name from the porch. "Phone call for you!"

"You coming?" Jerry asked, getting to his feet and dusting himself off.

"No, thanks. I'd like to follow the run down to the beach, see what I can find."

The kind old man went off but Mandy stayed, crawling through the bushes and glancing sideways to catch glimpses of the fancy new house next door. Painted pastel pink, with white balconies and gables, Moonshadow was enormous. Its wide windows glinted in the sun, and Mandy could see mosquito screens, striped blinds, and huge pots full of bright flowers. In the garden was a swimming pool surrounded by chairs and umbrellas, and on one of the loungers Mandy caught sight of a pair of tanned legs, a white bathing suit . . .

"What the . . . ?" A voice much closer to the fence stopped her in her tracks. A face stooped to peer at her. "What in heaven's name are you up to?"

Three

Mandy stayed down on all fours, peering into the impressive garden next door. The man who frowned at her through the white fence posts, a pair of garden shears in one hand, had fair hair and a neat mustache. His face had turned red from bending down.

"Mr. Miller?" she stammered.

His frown deepened.

"I'm Mandy Hope. I'm staying with the Logans. I'm looking for some raccoons."

She couldn't have chosen a worse thing to say. "Pure nuisances!" Robert Miller hissed. "We're overrun with the greedy, dirty things."

31

"Oh, but —"

Mr. Miller still squinted through the fence. "Are you English?"

Mandy nodded.

"I thought so. The English are all nuts about animals. No American would think twice about a raccoon."

"Mr. and Mrs. Logan like them," Mandy volunteered. This man's gruff voice had put her off her stride, but she gamely stood up for the unpopular animals. She wondered exactly what Mr. Miller had against them.

"I heard Bee Logan came over from Yorkshire." Mr. Miller stood up straight at last and came to peer over the fence with Mandy. He looked pleased to have proved his point. "Listen, if you get lucky and track down any of these raccoons, could you let me know?"

"What for?" Mandy felt she was right to be suspicious.

Robert Miller reached up to trim some overhanging branches off one of Jerry Logan's sea grapes. "Because I don't want them coming onto my land, that's for sure. This is some of the most expensive real estate in all of Florida, and I should know. I run the biggest real estate company on Blue Bayous. We don't intend to keep open house for a bunch of raccoons!"

With that, he turned on his heel and headed back toward the house, clipping some flowers with his shears, and tidying and smoothing the cream gravel on the paths as he went. When he reached the pool, Mandy saw the figure in the white bathing suit lean forward to talk to him. It was a girl of twelve or thirteen, with fair hair like her father.

"That's Courtney Miller," Joel said over Mandy's shoulder.

She jumped and turned. "Don't do that!"

"Still jumpy about the 'gator?" He grinned.

"Not at all." Mandy spent a few moments wondering about the girl next door. She looked about the same age as Mandy and Joel, but Mandy couldn't make out if she was shy or standoffish. In any case, she didn't look their way for Mandy to give her a friendly wave. What could Mandy do, except lose interest herself?

She turned back to Joel. "As a matter of fact, I'd forgotten all about the 'gator." Easing herself forward, she signaled for him to come deeper into the undergrowth.

"Grandma said to tell you lunch is ready, if you want some." He stood, hands on hips. "You missed one," he said, pointing to another raccoon print in the soil.

"So? I'm not hungry. I don't want any lunch, thanks."

"Please yourself." Joel shrugged and turned away. "She also asked, do you want to come to GRROWL with us after lunch?"

"To where?" Mandy didn't want to sound too interested. She'd an idea he'd said "growl," but this didn't make sense.

He ignored her question and ran off into the house, leaving her with her head stuck in the bushes, looking for raccoons.

Mandy did eventually find the creatures she was searching for. At one o'clock with the sun still at its highest, she had followed the raccoon run through the tangled undergrowth, out toward the seashore. The track came to an end among a thicket of spiky palm leaves and dense creepers, on mud banks that drained onto the beach.

She kept to the shade, wondering what to do next. Though she'd easily followed the tracks, they seemed now to have come to a dead end. *Maybe this means the raccoons never go farther than this point*, she thought. *Or maybe the waves have already washed their prints off the beach.* The water looked farther out than before, leaving a band of smooth white sand and heaps of shells stranded at the high watermark.

Mandy heard tiny movements in the bushes, and saw a pale crab scuttle along a mangrove root. Out on the beach, a heat haze shimmered.

And then she saw her raccoons. Two of them, mother and baby, stood ankle-deep in the muddy stream, their

backs toward her. Both held their ringed tails clear of
the water.

Mandy stood dead still, hardly daring to breathe. The
raccoons were only a few yards away. She could easily
make out the stout bodies with their short necks, and
the tips of their rounded ears. The mother was over half
a yard long, the baby much smaller. She could count six
stripes on the adult's tail.

If she crept to the side, she thought she would be able
to see more. The two raccoons were in a busy huddle,
turning something over between their fingers. Soon she
could see what it was: a glass jar with a metal lid that

had been carelessly thrown away. Perhaps it had washed up with the tide, and now the animals were determined to get at its contents.

They'll never do it, Mandy thought, creeping up on them without a sound. Now she could see the comical black masks of fur across their faces, their round, black button noses. To her surprise, the mother raccoon seemed to be able to unscrew the lid with her agile fingers. As soon as she had the jar open, she flung the lid into the mud and delved deep inside.

Whatever was in there tasted good to a raccoon. The mother offered the jar to the baby, who scooped out the sticky red stuff and licked his paw.

Mandy grinned to herself. The paws were so like hands, and the black masks gave them the air of two bandits raiding a bank. *Rita the raccoon.* She decided the name suited the mother. *And Ricky the baby.*

But Mandy was so gleeful at the sight of them that she grew careless. A twig snapped under her feet. In an instant, the raccoons vanished under the mangrove roots, leaving behind an empty jar and a silver lid glinting in the dappled sunlight.

"Over here we don't call a spade a spade," Bee Logan was explaining to Grandma Hope when Mandy finally made it back to Pelican's Roost. "We tend to cushion things in nice, soft phrases." She was closing the lid of a cardboard box that stood on a table out on the porch.

"I'm used to speaking my mind when necessary," Mandy's grandma countered.

It was the first time that Mandy had heard the two women disagree.

Her grandma was red in the face as she pushed on with her point of view. "And when I saw how hard she was chasing the poor thing, I'm afraid I couldn't hold my tongue!"

"What? Who?" Mandy dashed to join them. She peered into the box before the lid was fully closed, and caught sight of a little squirrel cowering in the bottom. "What happened?"

"I was taking a stroll at the bottom of the garden after lunch," Grandma explained, "minding my own business, enjoying the shade of the trees. I heard a noise in the next garden so I went to take a look. And what did I see but a girl in a white bathing suit chasing this poor little thing toward the fence!"

"That would be Courtney," Bee said. "We don't know her very well yet, but we guess she has the same frame of mind about the animals around here as her father does."

"What's wrong with it?" Mandy was worried. A squirrel would normally be able to outrun his pursuers and climb way out of reach into one of the tall pine trees at the garden's edge.

"One of his back legs is hurt." Grandma lifted the box and took it toward the Logans' truck. "He managed to squeeze through the fence into this garden before Miss Miller was able to lay hands on him. I picked him up and had words with the young lady, I can tell you!"

"She told her in no uncertain terms to stop chasing the squirrel and go back to her sunbathing by the pool," Bee Logan explained. "I guess no one's ever spoken to Courtney Miller like that before in her whole life!"

Then she must be pretty spoiled, Mandy thought. But she said nothing.

"I refuse to mince my words." With the squirrel safely installed in the back of the truck, Grandma smoothed out her crumpled shirt. "In my book, chasing an injured animal to within an inch of its life is downright cruel!"

"How did it hurt itself?" Mandy jumped into the back of the truck to hold the box steady.

"Can't say. Might have been caught in a trap." Bee Logan was climbing into the driver's seat. "We've left the men to do the dishes. We just have to wait for Joel, then we can go."

For a few minutes, Mandy sat waiting in the back of the Green Earth truck. Inside the cardboard box, the injured squirrel had gone quiet. He would be suffering from shock, she knew. Like her grandma, Mandy couldn't imagine how Courtney Miller could have been so cruel. Worse still, the girl next door was spying on them through the fence. Mandy caught sight of a sweep of blond hair, and a flash of white bathing suit.

"I won't be a sec," she told Gran and Bee, deciding at the spur of the moment to go and have it out with Courtney. She jumped out of the truck and headed for the fence.

"Don't be long!" Bee Logan looked at her watch. Then she saw where Mandy was headed. "Uh-oh, do you think that's a good idea?"

"Yep. Hang on!" She saw Courtney step back from the fence, then heard a woman's voice call from the house.

"Courtney, honey! Time for your dance class!"

Mandy reached the edge of the garden. "Hang on!" she cried. "I wanted to ask you something."

"Is it about the squirrel?" Courtney's voice sounded worried.

"Yes. Why were you chasing it?" Mandy went straight to the point. Close up, she saw that the girl was beautiful. Her eyes were light gray, her face freckled by the sun.

"I wasn't — well, I was, but I sure didn't mean . . ." She tailed off as her mother called again.

"Courtney, we have to go!"

She shook her head and backed off. "Sorry." The next moment she was running across the wide lawn toward the house.

"Well?" Grandma Hope asked when Mandy got back to the truck. She was still angry with Courtney over what she'd seen. "What did she say?"

"Nothing. She didn't have time." But now Mandy was even more curious. Courtney hadn't seemed the cruel type, that was for sure.

There was no chance to puzzle it out, however, as Joel came running out of Pelican's Roost at last. "Where are we going?" Mandy asked Bee.

"To GRROWL." She started the engine.

"Where?" This was what Joel had said earlier. Was it a place? How was it spelled? What did it mean?

"G-R-R-O-W-L. The Group for the Rescue and Rehabilitation of Wild Life. 'GRROWL' for short."

Joel vaulted into the truck beside Mandy, turning the peak of his white baseball cap around to the back of his head. "I asked you if you wanted to come, remember?" He seemed pleased to have scored another point in his game of one-upmanship with her.

"I thought you didn't care about wildlife?"

"Some animals are okay." He shrugged. Frowning, he refused to look at her as the truck lurched forward. "But I'm not like you, crazy about every living thing!"

"Want to bet?" Bee Logan laughed outright. "Why, only last year you came with me every single day to the rescue center!"

"That was last year," Joel mumbled.

Mandy was about to tease him, then thought better of it. So it *was* a tough-guy act she'd seen him put on earlier in the day! Maybe Joel thought it was uncool to admit how much he liked animals.

"So what does GRROWL do exactly?" Mandy asked Joel. She held on to the side of the truck with one hand and on to the box with the other as Joel's grandma went on up the bumpy drive.

"It's where Grandma works. Well, not so much 'works' as helps out. It's cool," he told her, overlooking his animals-are-boring line. "We take a twenty-minute drive up the island. GRROWL is this place in the middle of the wilderness area, where they take care of everything that gets run over by cars or shot at or trapped —"

"An animal hospital?" Mandy interrupted. This was the first she'd heard of it, though she'd been told that

Bee Logan felt about animals the same way as her husband, Jerry, did about native plants. It was what made Mandy like her the moment they met.

"Yep. They've got 'gators up there. And a vet, Lauren Young. She's cool, too."

They were well on the road at last, and the wind blew Mandy's fair hair back from her face.

Inside the box, they heard the squirrel begin to scratch, trying to get out. "Let's hope Lauren can help this one!" she breathed.

Four

They drove past the old-style wooden houses, painted yellow and aquamarine, with names like Sea Otter Cove and Bright Waters. Occasionally they would glimpse the sea beyond, and the heavy flight of pelicans as they waited for fish to rise close to the surface.

"I found two raccoons this afternoon," Mandy confessed to Joel above the hum of the engine. "They were amazing!"

Joel narrowed his eyes and gazed into the distance. This wasn't the time for him to show interest, but a question popped out anyway. "How big?"

"This big and this big." Mandy held her hand about

two feet from the floor of the truck, then lowered it to show him the size of Ricky. "Mother and baby."

"Alive?"

"Of course, alive!" This was a strange question, even for Joel. "Why?"

"Because you don't often see live ones." It was his turn to confess. "You usually see them squished by the side of the road. Most of the time, the live ones keep well out of sight."

"Poor things." Mandy was beginning to see that the life of your average raccoon was not an easy one. She felt the truck slow down and turn off the road down a narrow trail. "Are we here?" she asked.

"Pretty soon." Joel clung to the sides of the truck as it dipped and rocked over the rough ground.

They passed a worn sign with the initials GRROWL written in faded letters, and beneath them a cartoon drawing of a raccoon with a bandaged leg and his arm in a sling. Farther still down the track, they came to a group of big cages constructed of wood and wire netting to protect the center's injured animals and birds. Then, at the end of a bumpy two-mile drive, they reached the old wooden house where the hospital and visitors' center was based.

"Everybody out!" Bee Logan ordered from up front.

"Lauren will be expecting me to show up this afternoon to help out as usual, but she won't know about our new little patient back there."

"I'll go and tell her." Joel shot off ahead without waiting for Mandy.

"Okay, you pass me the box." Bee Logan asked her to lower it from the truck. "Your grandma tells me you do a lot of work with your folks back at Animal Ark," she said as they walked across the yard toward the building.

Mandy nodded and blushed. Mention of home gave her a twinge of homesickness. She didn't want to dwell on it, so she looked carefully at her new surroundings.

Unlike most of the quaint houses around here, the wooden boards of the rescue center had been left natural. They had seasoned to a pale gray color, and were twisted and warped out of shape so that the roof was uneven and the tall frame of stilts not quite level. Downstairs there was a small gift shop and information center for the visitors who came on Saturdays and Sundays. Upstairs on a balcony running around the outside of the building, a pale fawn Great Dane dog stared down at them.

Mandy took it all in, then smiled at Grandma. She felt better now about talking about Welford. "I help Mom and Dad in the clinic," she told Bee. "I want to be a vet when I finish school."

"Well, now's your chance to get a little more practical experience."

Mandy and Grandma let Bee go ahead with the box. They all went up the wooden stairs, to be greeted by the giant dog, who gave a deep, friendly bark, then sniffed at Bee's pockets.

"Hi, Duchess!" Bee said, pushing gently past.

Then Lauren Young, the vet at GRROWL, came out of an inner room with Joel. She was a lively, slim woman in her thirties, with long curly black hair, and dressed in blue shorts and a faded blue T-shirt. She said a quick "Hi," then took the box from Bee.

"Joel told me what happened." Lauren peered inside the box. "This looks like a Big Cypress fox squirrel we have here!"

"They're rare," Bee told them. "In fact they're on the endangered list."

"It's quite young." Lauren took the box inside and lifted the squirrel out. It struggled feebly, then lay limp in her hands, its splendid bushy tail hanging down. "The back leg's broken by the feel of it. Quite a lot of trauma to the wound, made by something sharp. Maybe a trap."

Mandy shuddered, then pulled herself together. "I can hold him if you want," she offered.

"Okay. We'll need antibiotics and a shot of anesthetic so we can make an X ray of the bone while he's out cold." She handed the trembling squirrel to Mandy, while Bee, Grandma Hope, and Joel left them to it. "I can see you're used to handling animals," she commented, busy opening cupboards to find what she needed.

Mandy nodded and put the squirrel down on a treatment table.

Though the house was old and ramshackle, the treatment room was clean and well equipped. And she could tell that, besides being a warm and friendly person, Lauren was an expert vet. Mandy held the patient while Lauren shaved a patch of fur from one of his front legs, injected first an anesthetic to put him to sleep, then the antibiotic to kill any infection. Soon the squirrel lay unconscious on the table.

"Well, the work we do here is all geared to getting these animals back into the wild," Lauren explained. "We run a telephone hotline and get cases from all over southern Florida. Right now we have a couple of deer, three otters, five skunks, twenty or so pelicans, and five alligators. With luck, more than fifty percent of these will be released."

"That's great." Mandy helped Lauren tape the squirrel's leg firmly to the X-ray table. They stood behind a screen and clicked a button. Then they went out to take the patient back into the first treatment room.

"We couldn't do it without the help of volunteers like Bee." Lauren waited and watched the squirrel put out its tongue and lick its top lip as the anesthetic began to wear off.

Studying the X-ray plate, Lauren decided that the fracture would soon heal. "We'll splint the leg and put off stitching the wound until the swelling's gone down," she said. "We'll keep him indoors for a couple of days, here in intensive care, until he gets over the shock, then we'll get him out into one of the enclosures. As soon as the bone is knitted back together, we can set him free here in the sanctuary. We have ten acres, so it's a nice, gradual return to the wild."

"You think he'll be okay?" Mandy watched the squirrel flick his tail and open his eyes. Lauren had a knack of making her feel relaxed and useful. A bit like her own mom, she thought.

"Yes. There's no reason why he shouldn't be among the lucky fifty percent." Lauren looked up with a smile. "I hear we have your grandma to thank?"

"My fighting grandma!" Mandy grinned back.

"Just like Bee. I can see why those two have been life-long friends." Lauren splinted the squirrel's leg and put him in a cage in a quiet corner of intensive care. "Why not get her to show you around?" she suggested to Mandy. "I'll finish up in here, then come and join you."

So Mandy went down to the yard and found the others busy cleaning out bird enclosures and hosing fresh water into the troughs where the deer drank. The timid animals shied away from human contact, and huddled in a corner as Bee went quietly about her business.

"I come here most afternoons," she told Mandy, closing the gate after her, taking fresh straw to the small animal enclosures and tending to the rabbits and skunks. "I like to do as much as I can. Jerry tells me I do too much, but I say if I didn't do it, who would? The center's short of money as it is. They couldn't possibly afford to pay someone to do this kind of work."

Mandy helped clean the floor of the rabbit hutches while the occupants came out and sunned themselves in their enclosure. They sat and twitched their ears, then hopped to nibble at lettuce leaves that Joel and Dorothy pushed through the netting.

"Anyhow, I tell Jerry he's not the one to talk about doing too much!" Bee chatted on. "He's nearly seventy-five and he refuses to give up his gardening business! Mind you, I do sometimes agree with him that this rescue work isn't for us senior citizens."

"But you don't look old!" Mandy protested. Both Bee and Jerry behaved like youngsters. "It must be the healthy Florida air!"

Bee smiled, finished with the rabbits, and told Mandy to follow her out into the yard. "It's all very well dealing with rabbits and deer," she explained, leading on to an enclosure with a pool, surrounded by rocks and bushes.

"Where are we now?" Mandy turned around slowly, looking for the animals who lived here. The water in the pool was murky, there were logs and debris floating in it, and flattened areas among the bushes where something large lay and sunned itself.

Bee Logan gave a mischievous grin and pointed at a sign to the left of the entrance. She closed the gate with a click after them.

Mandy read the notice, which said DO NOT FEED THE ALLIGATORS. She spun around to protest, but Bee was already busy raking up dead leaves into a plastic sack. And now that she looked more closely, the logs in the muddy water weren't logs at all. They had nostrils and eyes; they had scales and legs that waddled onto the banks.

"This is what Jerry means about it being a young person's job," Bee went on. "Deer and skunks are fine for old folks like me. But when an alligator decides to charge at ten miles per hour, you need to get out of his way pretty quick!"

"Meet Allie." After she'd shown Mandy around the enclosure, Bee Logan introduced her to an alligator that they kept all by himself in a special pen.

The great creature shifted and hauled himself farther

into the sun. Though a strong wire fence separated them, Mandy took a step back.

"Allie isn't one of our success stories," Bee explained. They'd finished shoveling dead leaves into sacks and come to take a quick look at the segregated alligator.

"How come?" Mandy thought that Allie looked strong and healthy, ready to return to the mangrove swamps at any time.

"He's one of these nuisance 'gators." Bee got busy. She took a hunk of red meat out of another sack and hooked it onto a spike that was connected to a wire pulley.

Looking more closely, Mandy saw that the strong wire was slung low across Allie's pool. "You mean, he would attack humans?"

"That's right." Bee worked a lever and the meat swung out across the water. "Not his fault of course. But if tourists ignore the signs and go ahead and feed these guys, what can you expect?"

As the pulley whirred and the meat hung suspended, they watched Allie slowly turn his head. He heaved himself to the water's edge and suddenly launched himself. There was a tremendous splash, a mighty flick of his tail, and he was surging through the pond toward his supper. He reached it and lunged clear of the water, his mighty jaws snapping.

"He missed!" Mandy whispered, her gaze fixed on the swirling water where Allie had landed and vanished.

"Here he comes again!" Bee said. They watched him rise a second time. This time the jaws opened and clutched the meat. He dragged it down from the spike and surged off with it, making a tidal wave in the small pool.

Mandy breathed out. "What'll happen to him in the end?" If Allie couldn't be trusted to go back into the wild, would he have to stay at GRROWL forever?

"We're trying to fix him up with a new home," Bee told her, working the lever to pull the spike back to dry land.

"But who'd want to adopt an alligator?" Mandy was still staring at Allie. By now he'd reached the opposite bank with his chunk of meat and was greedily devouring it. His teeth tore at the flesh, which he shook and ripped apart.

"Exactly." Bee, too, watched carefully. "Not your average household pet, eh? Normally with injured 'gators, we treat them, then release them into our sanctuary. Pretty soon they travel out into the wilderness, good as new. But Allie needs a special environment; somewhere where he's not going to bump up against tempting, unsuspecting tourists. So Lauren's been calling the zoos and theme parks to see if they can take him."

"You mean, he'll have to spend the rest of his life in a zoo?" Mandy cried. This didn't seem fair. She pictured him cooped up in a cage, bored and lonely.

"We don't know yet. But some zoos are fine. They give the 'gators plenty of space. And theme parks are even better. There, the 'gators wouldn't even know the difference. They have lakes to swim in, and the grounds are landscaped to be as natural as possible. Ask Jerry. He's done work in some of them."

The problem of Allie preyed on Mandy's mind for the rest of the afternoon. Even when Lauren Young came down to announce that the fox squirrel had recovered well from his anesthetic, Mandy couldn't help wondering about poor Allie. She mentioned him to Joel on the ride back to Pelican's Roost.

"Is a theme park here like one of our safari parks back home?" she asked. "I mean, would there be lots of animals, with visitors driving through at a distance?"

"Sure."

"So it'd be better than a zoo?"

"Sure." He bit into a bar of candy which he'd picked up in the gift shop at GRROWL, even though it was closed until the weekend.

"Well, let's hope Lauren can find him a place in one," she sighed. She grabbed the side of the truck as it bounced over a bump in the road.

"She already did," Joel told her carelessly, through bits of peanut and chocolate. "They're going to take him over to Ibis Gardens in a couple of days."

Mandy gritted her teeth. "You never said!" Joel was back to his maddening couldn't-care-less style. Was it on purpose or by accident that he made her feel as if her questions were a boring nuisance to him?

"You never asked," he replied, flinging the candy wrapper out of the truck and watching it fly on the wind.

Five

"In this state we have a three-hundred-dollar fine for dropping litter." Joel's grandmother told Joel off when they got back home. She'd seen the wrapper whisk away into the gutter, stopped the truck, and made him walk back to collect it. Now he was sulking.

"Folks around here take pride in stuff like that." Jerry Logan was setting off sprinklers to water the plants after the day's heat. "You're not in the city now!"

Mandy noticed that Joel did at least have the grace to look embarrassed.

"Sorry." He looked around for a means of escape and spotted it next door. "Hey, Courtney!" he called through the fence.

"Do you want to come and swim?" the girl called back.

Joel disappeared inside the house to collect his swimming things, then ran off up the drive without asking Mandy if she wanted to come, too.

Bee Logan shook her head and sighed, "Whatever happened to our sweet little grandson?"

"He grew up," Jerry said.

"No, he just thinks he did," she countered. "We're still waiting for the real thing."

Mandy said she didn't mind about the swimming, though she was still curious about Courtney's reason for chasing the poor squirrel. But with Joel blowing hot and cold all the time, she felt it was best to keep out of his way. "I'd rather go to the beach," she told them. The sun was about to go down. She wanted to track raccoons down the run, to see if she could find Rita and her baby again.

So Mandy went off by herself, picking up trails. She recognized where the raccoons had stopped to feed from the flattened grass and scattered pieces of crab shell. She found a stream of running water and more footprints on the bank, then two full-grown raccoons squatting waist-deep in the stream.

What now? Mandy was learning that raccoons didn't usually do what she expected. These two stood so still with the water swirling around them, they looked like statues. She watched for several minutes before she found out the answer to her silent question.

Splash! One raccoon lashed out with his front paw. He scooped a fish out of the water and bashed it hard against a nearby stone. Supper!

Mandy looked more closely. There were many fish swimming through the reeds. The raccoons had waded in and simply waited until one of the fish brushed against their legs. Then *wham!* The sharp claws struck. Fish was on the menu.

She grinned at the sight. This wasn't Rita and her baby, but these raccoons were cute and clever like them. And now the sun really was setting low over the sea, touching the horizon and melting like liquid gold. Mandy knew that soon darkness would fall, so she turned back and headed for home, leaving the raccoons to their evening feast.

At Pelican's Roost, the grown-ups were rolling back the years, chatting about old times. There was no sign of

Joel, but Mandy's grandma told her he was still next door with Courtney.

"Why not go and join them?" she asked.

Mandy shook her head. "They don't want me around." Joel and Courtney seemed to get along well, and now that she came to think about it, this could be one of the reasons why he was being so weird.

After all, if Courtney Miller and her parents didn't like the wildlife around here, and Joel wanted to impress her, he would try to take the same side as them. *A pity*, Mandy thought with a sigh.

"Sure?" Grandma looked concerned.

"Yes. I think I'll take a book up to bed and go to sleep early," she decided. "Or maybe write a postcard to James."

Her best friend from Welford would really love to be here. She went upstairs, picturing how they could have shared the excitement over the alligators, dolphins, egrets, squirrels, pelicans, raccoons . . .

No good thinking about it, she decided. And, anyway, she wanted to be awake early, out on the raccoon trail once more. She would take her camera and shoot close-ups of them dipping their food in the water, catch the fresh looks on their bandit faces, show them perched on mangrove roots or clambering through the trees.

So she turned on her bedside lamp. She slid the mosquito screen back and stepped out onto the balcony, lounging on the banister and gazing out over the feathery palm trees toward the sea. From next door, she could hear the yells from Joel and Courtney as they played in the floodlit pool. Otherwise, dusk had brought peace and quiet to this corner of Blue Bayous Island.

Eventually, the bugs drove the two swimmers inside the house.

"Ouch! I just got bitten!" Courtney's voice wailed.

"Me, too."

"Now I'll be covered with awful red bumps!"

The splashing stopped and Mandy saw two dripping figures wrapped in towels make their way into the big mansion. *Fast food!* Mandy grinned to herself, describing the way the bugs had just made a meal of Joel and Courtney.

She was tired. Her bed was white and inviting inside the darkened room, so she went in, pulled back the sheet, put her unopened book under the pillow, and slid between the covers. Within minutes, she was fast asleep.

Rattle-scrabble-rattle! Feet scampered over the roof. Mandy woke with a start in the middle of the night.

Maybe she'd dreamed it. In the dark room she could

hear a clock ticking, but nothing else. She turned over to go back to sleep.

Scratch-scuffle-scratch!

There it was again. This time Mandy sat bolt upright. The noise was real. It sounded like animals scuttling about up there. Raccoons on the roof!

Quickly she flung off the bedclothes and fumbled her way toward the balcony. Silver moonlight guided her, and as she slid back the screen, her eyes grew used to the dark. She stepped out in her bare feet and craned her neck to try and peer onto the top of the house.

Two raccoons blinked down at her from the edge of the roof.

"Rita!" she breathed. "Ricky!"

Rita twitched her ears and white whiskers. She poked her face toward the person who had disturbed their nighttime ramblings. Her eyes were surrounded by black fur like a panda, and there was a stripe of black running from the center of her nose up onto her forehead, making her look as if she was frowning down at Mandy.

It was the same mother raccoon and her baby, Mandy was sure. The youngster was the right size. He stayed nervously at his mother's side. "Wait here!" she whispered gently, tiptoeing along the balcony and down the wooden stairs to ground level. When she looked back up at the roof, the two raccoons were still watching her.

Mandy headed for the kitchen and Bee Logan's store of dried fruit. Under her bare feet the old wooden floorboards creaked and groaned. She took a pile of dried apricots and a dish of cool water outside again and set them down at the edge of the porch. Then she sat on one of the cane rocking chairs and waited.

With luck, the raccoons would spot the treat and scramble down from the roof. Minutes ticked by without movement, but Mandy was patient. She sat in the moonlight, looking up at the stars. Not far away the waves broke on the shore.

Then she heard the hard rattling of claws on wooden boards. They were going to risk it after all. Rita's face appeared, peering down from the porch roof at the pieces of fruit beside the dish. Soon she came scrambling down a post, her ringed tail waving, her black nose twitching and sniffing.

Mandy held her breath. The raccoon's brown-gray coat looked more silver in this light. Her dumpy body landed on the ground. She looked up and let her baby know that it was safe to follow. With one eye on Mandy, they crept forward to take the treat.

Their little hands seized the apricots, their sharp teeth sank into them. They wiped sticky bits from their whiskers. Then they decided to dip the food into the water, dabbling and paddling it until it softened and fell apart. Rita put her head to one side. What had happened to the solid fruit? She scooped her hand into the water and sieved out the soggy pieces, making the best of what she could rescue. Quickly she stuffed the food into her mouth.

Mandy grinned, watching the little one follow suit. If

only she had her camera. But no; she wouldn't be able
to take a picture without using the flash, and that would
have scared the raccoons away. What she wanted was
for them to come back again whenever they felt like it.
She wanted to make friends with these two beautiful,
furry creatures, to win their trust and show them that
not all humans were their enemies.

Meanwhile, she sat in her rocking chair, feeling the
breeze in her hair, watching Rita and Ricky devour one
of the best midnight feasts of their lives.

The sunny days at Pelican's Roost rolled seamlessly by.
Mandy fell into the nightly habit of putting out food for
Rita and Ricky, who came to expect the secret treat.
Then, from dawn to dusk Mandy was outdoors, helping
Jerry Logan and her grandpa with gardening jobs, visit-
ing GRROWL with Bee and Grandma, and sometimes,
whenever Joel was in a good mood, she would just hang
out with him.

The two of them would scour the beach for unusual
shells: cockles and oysters, cat's paws and shark's eyes.
Joel said he had a shell collection at home in New York.

"I've got sand dollars," he told her. "You don't see
them too often, but I've got six." He described the flat
shells with a star marking and five narrow slits. "Blue

Bayous is famous for shells. Here's a sunray venus!" He stooped to pick up a shiny pink shell.

"How come you know so much about them?" Mandy was impressed. For a change, Joel wasn't teasing or ignoring her, the two things he did most often when she was around. Especially when Courtney Miller called for him to go over to Moonshadow, she noticed.

"Grandpa used to bring me down here and teach me the names. Every summer I took a whole sackful home with me. My mom said I'd brought the whole beach back."

"She didn't mind?" Mandy looked out for the round, white sand dollars to add to her own collection.

"Nope. She reckoned it was better than crabs and frogs and other things I wanted to bring home."

"I knew it!" Mandy grinned. It was her turn to tease. "I knew you really liked animals!" Every time Joel went along to GRROWL, she would catch him sneaking a look at the injured squirrel or playing with Duchess, Lauren Young's friendly Great Dane.

"Yeah, yeah." He shrugged. "I was a weird kid. You want to know something?"

Mandy picked up a cone-shaped shell and slipped it into her pocket. "What?"

"You won't tell Courtney?" he checked with her.

"Why not?"

"She'd say it was strange. Her folks don't think the same way as my grandparents do about life here on the island."

Mandy frowned. "Well, I'm not likely to tell her, am I?" Courtney had made it pretty clear that she wanted nothing to do with Mandy. "So go ahead."

"There was one time I made this plan to take a pet home, along with the shells. I figured I could hide it in the same sack and keep it in our apartment. I was going to feed it peanut butter and cookies and hide it in my room in case my mom said I couldn't keep it." He grinned shyly at her.

"What kind of pet was it?"

Joel cleared his throat. "Sure you won't tell?"

"Certain!" She flashed him an impatient look.

"A baby raccoon," he mumbled.

"A raccoon?" She opened her eyes wide.

"Yeah, well, I was only a little kid."

"I thought you said no one in America was interested in raccoons! Anyway, what happened?"

"There was this one little guy, about six months old. I called him Ricky —"

"Wait! Ricky? That's what I've decided to call *my* raccoon. The young one that uses the roof at Pelican's

Roost as part of his run." The coincidence made her warm even more to Joel's story.

"Well, my Ricky used to come right into the house and take food out of my hand. He was real tame. So the last night before I was due to fly back to New York, I waited for him to come in and when no one was looking I made a grab for him." He grinned again at the memory.

"What happened?"

"Ricky didn't like the look of the sack. He kicked out and gave me one heck of a bite. I yelled out loud, Grandpa came running, and little Ricky scooted out the window. They had to give me a tetanus shot, just in case." Joel sighed. "I don't think he would have liked New York, either!"

"Now I'll tell you something." Mandy decided to trust Joel with her secret. "These last few nights I've been putting food out for Ricky and his mom."

"Do they come and get it?"

She nodded. "Down from the roof, right onto the porch. Would you like to come and see?"

"Maybe." Instead of showing interest, Joel shrugged and wandered off.

Puzzled and hurt, Mandy watched him go. *I get it!* she said to herself suddenly, then followed quickly. "So, it was okay to like raccoons and frogs and things a couple of summers ago, but not now! Now raccoons are a nuisance. They're just pests. They're boring!"

He sniffed and walked on. "Yeah, well . . ."

"This couldn't by any chance have something to do with Courtney Miller, could it?" Mandy ran ahead and made him stop.

"Are you crazy?"

"Courtney doesn't like raccoons, does she? And you have to follow everything she says!"

He turned on her. "You don't know anything!"

"Yes, I do. Or I can guess. The whole Miller family would like Blue Bayous to be a wildlife-free zone!"

Now she was really angry. Her ideas ran wild as she flung accusations at Joel. "Her father doesn't like raccoons, either. Did you ever stop to think how that poor little squirrel injured his leg?" she demanded. "You want to know what my theory is? I think Mr. Miller set traps for raccoons in his precious garden, and the squirrel got caught by mistake!"

"So?" Joel glared back. "It's their land. They have every right to keep it clear of pests. Raccoons carry rabies, or didn't you know that?"

"You sound like Mr. Miller!" she challenged, her eyes blazing with anger. She'd gone further than she intended, said things she shouldn't have said. She had no evidence that there were traps in the garden next door, except Lauren Young's opinion about the squirrel's injury. *Maybe a trap*, she'd said.

Joel stared, then sidestepped her. He stormed off up the beach. "You know what?" He flung a final remark over his shoulder. "I think you'd better stop feeding those two raccoons, or else . . . !"

"Or else what?" Mandy wished she could unsay what she'd just said. She should never have told Joel about Rita and Ricky. Now she ran after him, trying to catch hold of his arm.

He shrugged her off, his threat hanging unfinished in the air. "Just don't encourage them, that's all. It's not safe."

"What do you mean, 'not safe'? How do you know? What's going on?" Mandy ran after him through the soft, warm sand. He knew more than he was saying, she was sure.

But Joel was like a shell himself now, an oyster or a clam, with his mouth firmly shut and his eyes narrowed. He walked off without looking back, leaving her standing on the beach, wondering what on earth his threat could mean.

Six

"Tact and diplomacy," Grandpa Hope advised when Mandy told him her problem. "That's what I would try now."

She had come to him for advice. She knew her grandfather would see all angles, maybe even be able to explain what had gotten into Joel.

She watched Grandpa hoe the loose soil around the sea grapes in the Logans' garden, wearing a bright blue shirt and white shorts. Even on vacation her grandpa liked to keep busy in the garden. "What do you mean exactly?" she asked.

"Well, instead of having these fights with Joel and refusing to get to know this girl from next door, why not take things a bit more gently?" He looked up and smiled at her. "You know what your problem is, Mandy? You take it for granted that everyone thinks the way you do!"

"Do I?"

Grandpa laughed. "Yes, don't sound so surprised. Most of us do it all of the time without realizing it." He rested on the long shaft of his hoe and studied Mandy's face. "What do you actually know about Courtney?" he asked gently.

"Not much. Only that she doesn't want to know me!" Ever since Mandy had tried to talk to her about the injured squirrel, Courtney had gone out of her way to avoid her. "And that no one in her family likes raccoons!" Mr. Miller had called them greedy, dirty nuisances. "And you know what's even worse?"

"What?" Grandpa Hope looked thoughtful as he got back to work with the hoe.

"The Millers are turning Joel against animals, too." She explained about his recent threat against the raccoons. "And that was after I trusted him, too," she said sadly. "Because, deep down, I think he really does care!"

"That's a hard one," Grandpa agreed. Then he had an idea. "Listen, Mandy, if you want to convert someone who doesn't care for animals into someone who's as crazy about them as you are, perhaps you should persuade that person to come along to Bee's Rescue Center sometime."

"You mean Courtney?"

"Yes. Let her see for herself the sort of work that goes on around here to protect the wildlife."

"Hang on. You mean, actually invite Courtney Miller to GRROWL?" Mandy's mouth fell open.

"Yes. Why not?" Grandpa Hope made it sound perfectly possible. "Didn't I overhear you say you were going up there later today?"

"No way! She won't even talk to me . . . She completely ignores me whenever she gets the chance . . . She and Joel don't want to know!" It was hard enough to be left out like this without being the one to try and make things right. In any case, today was the day when Lauren Young planned to take Allie to his new home at Ibis Gardens. She'd promised to take Mandy and Joel along, too.

"How do you know?"

"I just know."

Her grandpa carried on with his gardening. "See, you're jumping to conclusions. Have you actually spoken to Courtney since we got here?"

"Only once. Just after Grandma told her off!"

"What did she say?"

Mandy racked her brains. "Not much. Her mom called her. Oh, yes, she said sorry."

"See!"

"No, but . . ." She felt herself blush. "I don't know what she was sorry about."

"Have you tried to find out?"

"No, but . . ." Finally she came up with the same reason as before. "It's like I said, Courtney doesn't want to talk to me."

"Hmm. So it's war?" Grandpa Hope leaned his hoe against a tree.

"I think that the Millers have set traps to catch the raccoons," Mandy pointed out. She intended to keep on feeding them and encouraging them to use the run, come what may. "But the raccoons are great, Grandpa. They were here long before people came and settled. And they're really clever. I saw one open a screwtop jar the other day. Honestly!"

"That's really something," he admitted, looking up at the sun and deciding to go indoors. "Are you sure about the traps?" he asked.

"No, but I wouldn't put it past Mr. Miller. He hates them. And there was that squirrel who was injured in their garden. And now there's this warning from Joel that feeding Rita and Ricky isn't safe!"

"Come inside and tell your grandma and Bee about

it," Grandpa Hope suggested. He put his arm around Mandy's shoulder and led her toward the house. "If there are traps set next door, I agree with Joel; the run certainly isn't safe for the poor unsuspecting raccoons!"

"It's not against the law." Bee Logan's face was creased into a deep frown. "If folks want to trap raccoons, they can bring in pest control people to do it for them and there's not a thing we can do."

Jerry Logan shook his head. "Up until now it hasn't been a problem on Blue Bayous. Live and let live, we always say. But we've got a lot of new houses going up. We get thousands of snowbirds flying south for the winter and deciding to put down roots for good."

"Snowbirds?" Grandma Hope asked.

"Retired folks like you and Tom," he explained. "They don't like the cold winters in Chicago or New York, so they buy vacation homes down here. Problem is, they generally like their nature pretty tame, and when raccoons sneak in and steal their fruit or dig up their flower beds, they get pretty mad."

Mandy listened hard. This fit in with the Millers' reaction, she knew.

"We even get folks calling the Center, asking us to get rid of them!" Bee tapped the table with her car keys. "I turn right around and tell them that at GRROWL we want to *save* raccoons, not *kill* them. That soon hushes them up!"

Jerry looked at his watch and reminded them of the time. "Didn't I hear you say that Joel wants to take that trip to Ibis Gardens with you this afternoon?" he asked.

So Mandy went to find him while Bee Logan turned the truck in the drive. Her grandparents had decided to stay at home with Jerry, who planned to take them fishing off Pine Island.

"Joel?" she called upstairs, then out on the back porch. There was no sign of him. She went down the garden, still calling. Then she spotted him through the fence, lounging by the pool with Courtney. They were both wearing headphones, listening to music by the look of it.

Mandy swallowed hard and took a deep breath. *Tact and diplomacy*, she told herself. She would have to cut up the drive, through the gate at Moonshadow, and across the lawn to attract Joel's attention. "Here goes!" she muttered.

"Joel!" Mandy went through the garden, right up to the pool. She had to shout. "We're leaving now. Do you still want to come?"

He took off the headphones and looked up from a magazine. "Where to?"

"Ibis Gardens," she reminded him.

Joel shrugged. "Maybe." He glanced sideways at Courtney to judge her reaction.

"We have to go right now. Your grandma's waiting." Mandy felt Courtney's stare boring into her. Her mouth turned down at the corners, and she kept her headphones firmly over her ears, deliberately cutting out what Mandy was saying. *Tact and diplomacy*, she repeated to herself. "Would you like to come, too?" she asked.

Courtney stopped swaying her shoulders to the beat and took off the headphones. "Sorry, I didn't get that."

Mandy repeated the invitation. "We're going to Ibis Gardens. Would you like to come?"

"What is this place?" Courtney turned from Mandy to Joel.

"Theme park," he explained, very noncommittal.

"You mean water slides and film studios?"

"More of a jungle kind of theme park."

"Like a safari?" Courtney still sounded interested. "Elephants and lions and tigers?"

Joel nodded. "Gorillas and 'gators."

She flicked her blond hair behind her shoulder. "Are you sure you want me to come along?" she asked Mandy.

Taken aback, Mandy nodded. "If you want to come." She'd expected Courtney to give an outright "no."

"It's just that I got this idea that you didn't like me — because of the squirrel!"

Mandy felt her face go red. "I've been meaning to ask you what happened there," she confessed.

"And I guess I've been wanting to tell you!"

They both gave an embarrassed grin. "I wasn't chasing him exactly," Courtney explained. "I know that's what it looked like —"

"That's what my grandma thought." Mandy decided to try and help her out. To her surprise, Courtney seemed shy. She kept on stumbling over her words. "So what really happened?"

"In a way it was my fault. It's my dad. He found out the squirrel kept coming into the attic, so he bought a trap from the hardware store."

Mandy frowned. They'd been right about this much, then.

"I didn't want him to do it, but he went ahead anyway." Again Courtney hesitated.

Mandy noticed Joel hanging back, his eyes wide, his mouth half open. This was obviously a side of Courtney he hadn't seen before, either. "And the squirrel got caught in the trap?"

She nodded. "I was in my studio, practicing." She glanced up and met Mandy's stare. "My dance studio is up on the first floor," she explained. "My mom wants me to be a dancer, just like her. So, I'm training at the *barre* and I hear this noise up in the attic. I go up and find the little squirrel. He was making a squealing noise. I couldn't bear it, so I lifted the trap and let him go."

"And he ran away?" Mandy guessed the next part. "Out of the house, down into the garden. You went after him to see how badly hurt he was, and that's when Grandma saw you?"

Courtney sighed. "Right."

"Why didn't you say that?" It was Mandy's turn to stammer and stumble.

"I tried, remember? But I knew it looked real bad, and I thought you hated me for it." She hung her head.

"Okay, okay!" Joel broke in at last and grabbed Courtney by the arm. "Let me get this straight. You like animals? Is that what this means?"

"I don't know much about them, but yes, I guess I do!"

"Wow!" He turned to Mandy, relief spreading across his face. "How wrong can you be?"

"Not much wronger!" she admitted. She felt relief flood through her. But now they had to get a move on if they were to get to Ibis Gardens before dinnertime. "So, how about it?" she asked Courtney. "Do you want to come with us?"

"Sure, why not?" she answered with a beaming smile.

*   *   *

"Look at the line!" Lauren Young pointed to the long line
of people waiting to go into the theme park. They drove
through a side entrance in the GRROWL truck, with Allie safely sedated and locked inside a strong crate. Bee
Logan had stayed to take care of things at the Rescue
Center, while Lauren, Mandy, Joel, and Courtney drove
the alligator to his new home.

"I'm glad we don't have to wait," Courtney said. "I
hate any place where you have to line up."

One or two people glanced inside the truck as they
passed. They read the DO NOT TOUCH notice on Allie's
crate, and glimpsed his scaly back and sharp teeth.
There were a few "Wow!"s and a couple of men with
cameras taking pictures. For a few moments, the
GRROWL truck was the center of attention.

Then they were inside the theme park, into a different world, a whole new continent. Jungle creepers
trailed across the path from branch to branch of trees
with broad, shiny leaves. Mandy thought she recognized giant figs, mahogany trees, and palms. A waterfall
tumbled down rocks into a deep pool between huge
ferns and bright flowers.

"All those rocks are fake," Joel informed them,
adding that he'd been here many times before. "And you
see that steam coming up from the ground?"

Mandy noticed small jets of moist air blowing through the undergrowth.

"That's fake, too, to make it feel like a real jungle. And you hear those birds in the trees?"

She listened. "Fake?" she sighed.

He nodded. "On audiotape."

"Only in America!" Lauren laughed, watching Mandy's stunned expression. "Good, isn't it?"

"Real good!" Courtney broke in. "All the stuff you get in Africa without the bother of flying over there."

She'd been chatting all the way from the Rescue Center, telling Lauren about her life. Mandy had heard that it was Courtney's mother's ambition for her to go to dance school in New York, and that Moonshadow was their summer home. They'd had the studio built especially for her. Her mother made her take her training seriously, she said. "Two hours a day, even during vacation."

"How about you?" Lauren put her finger on the important question. "Do you enjoy it?"

There was a pause while Courtney shrugged. "I guess so."

Mandy listened mostly in silence. Girls like Courtney usually scared her. They seemed to know everything, and to have everything they wanted. It made her want to keep quiet about her own life in England; what would Courtney possibly want to know about being a vet's daughter in a small Yorkshire village?

"See the gorillas?" Lauren slowed the truck as they passed another landscaped area set back from the path and separated by a deep, rocky moat full of clear water.

The huge compound was overgrown, the steam rising thickly from the ground like mist. Then, through the leaves and tall grass, about a hundred yards off, Mandy spotted two gorillas. They turned their heads at the sound of the truck and watched Mandy's group watching them.

"Amazing!" Courtney cried. She craned out of the truck for a better view. "Look at their faces! They're so — human!"

Mandy stared at the two enormous creatures. Their black faces wore the expressions of wise old men under jutting brows. Their shoulders and chests were massive. Yet they picked with delicate fingers at the fruit left scattered around by keepers. They examined it carefully, put it into their mouths, and chewed slowly.

She could have stayed there for ages, watching the gorillas watching them. What were they thinking? Did they mind being stared at? Did they ever think of home?

"It's kind of sad," Courtney said quietly.

"How come?" Joel still kept up part of the old act, but now it was for the benefit of both Mandy and Courtney. He made it clear he'd seen it all before, lolling back in his seat, chewing gum.

"I don't know how to explain. They must feel like freaks."

"I know what you mean," Mandy said quickly. "How would *we* feel if someone stuck *us* in a compound?"

"Sure. I mean, nobody asked them if they wanted to be here." She fell silent and sat back beside Joel as Lauren drove on.

Slowly they wove their way through the crowds, past elephants and giraffes on mock African plains. The giraffes stretched their long necks to reach tender shoots from the tops of trees, ignoring the crowds. But the elephants came close, waving their trunks and trundling forward for treats that never came. DO NOT FEED THE ANIMALS it said on small, regular notices along the side of the trail.

They drove on, then stopped again to look at small brown-and-white deer in the animal nursery, and golden pythons and lizards in the reptile house. It was here that Lauren met up with her friend, the alligator keeper, Jeff Kent.

"Hi. How are you all doing?" he asked, striding down the side of the truck to check on Allie. The keeper was a young black man in a smart green shirt and tan trousers. He hopped up into the back beside the alligator crate. Then he yelled out directions for Lauren to drive on to the alligator pool.

"Straight ahead!" he instructed. "Okay, now, take a left past the tigers!"

"Tigers!" Courtney craned to look. "See that white one over there! Gee, I never saw a white tiger before!"

Mandy couldn't help staring at her. It was taking time to get rid of the old version of Courtney Miller and get used to this new one. This Courtney said she didn't know much about animals, but each one she saw made her gasp with wonder.

"Take a right past Monkey Island," Jeff told Lauren. "Almost there," he promised.

"Monkeys!" Courtney was like a small child, bouncing on her seat, pointing at the animals' acrobatics as lemurs, gibbons, and chimps swung from branch to branch. "Oh, aren't they adorable?"

It was time to pull over beside the alligator pool and for Jeff to unhitch the tailgate of the truck. They piled out to help.

From his cramped cage in the back of the truck, Allie snorted and rattled at the door.

"Come on, Mandy, help us out." Lauren broke into her thoughts. They had a job to do. "This 'gator is getting hungry and bored. And the crate's way too heavy for the pair of us to handle!"

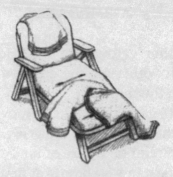

Seven

"Never get any closer than five yards to an alligator!" Jeff Kent quoted the golden rule.

"As if!" Courtney stood back and watched them move Allie's crate into position inside the compound.

"Especially if, like poor Allie here, he has what you might call an attitude problem," Lauren added, herding Joel and Mandy back behind the fence.

"Look, here he comes!" Mandy warned. Jeff had lifted the door of the crate and stood clear. The 'gator crawled out slowly, lumbering onto the sandy bank at the edge of the pool. He swished his tail, raising a cloud of dust as he went.

"Won't the other 'gators fight him?" Joel asked. There were at least six others in the compound; some in the water, some on the far bank.

"Maybe." Jeff cast an expert eye over Allie's thick, knobbly hide, his stout legs, and vicelike jaws. "But I think this fellow can take care of himself."

"There may be a few standoffs at first. But they'll settle down soon enough," Lauren agreed.

"Hey, Mandy, look at this!" Courtney pulled her to one side as the others concentrated on Allie's progress into the water. "Are these lizards, or what?"

She pointed to two small creatures with yellow stripes, hiding in a clump of saw grass nearby. Their long tails and hind legs trailed in the pool, but their heads and short front legs rested clear of the water on a hot, dry stone.

Mandy looked closely. Though they were only thirty inches long from head to tail, they were perfect miniatures of Allie. "No, they're baby 'gators!" she gasped.

Lauren Young heard the excited cry and strode across. "Yep," she confirmed. "You want to hold one?"

Mandy nodded, but she bit her lip and held her breath as the vet approached one of the baby alligators from behind and clamped one hand firmly around his jaw. Lauren strapped the jaw together with a firm band of tape before handing him over to Mandy.

"Won't that hurt him?" Courtney whispered.

"No. He won't mind. You can stroke him if you like."

Mandy held the baby alligator tightly. His yellow skin was smooth and dry, his tiny claws razor-sharp. The eyes were set close on top of his head, and his expression was glazed and blank.

"Which way?" Courtney held back, her hand trembling slightly.

"From head to tail," Lauren instructed.

Courtney stroked the baby alligator nervously.

"Does he like it?" Mandy asked. This was so weird.

She had no way of telling if the creature was angry or not. His poor mouth looked odd clamped shut with a strong tape. "I think we should put him back now," she whispered to Courtney.

So Lauren unstrapped his jaw and plopped him back into the shallow water. "Jeff's really pleased with these two babies. They were hatched here at Ibis Gardens."

Mandy noticed a fully grown alligator floating gently toward them, only the eyes and nostrils above water.

"The hot sun incubates the eggs," she explained. "Then, when the babies hatch, the mother takes care of them for several months. They make good parents."

By this time, Allie had heaved himself into the pool and was exploring the banks. "Why don't you all go for some ice cream?" Jeff suggested, happy with the way things had gone. "There's an ice cream parlor by the deer nursery."

So they left Lauren and the keeper to settle Allie in and trooped off for cold drinks and ice cream. They sat out of the sun under some tall pine trees, watching the monkeys at play in the distance. Other kids strolled by with their parents and grandparents, going to feed the donkeys and the warthogs, or lining up for a boat trip around Monkey Island.

"You know something . . ." Courtney began.

"I wanted to ask you . . ." Mandy jumped in at the same time. "No, sorry, you go!"

"No, it's okay." A blush spread over Courtney's fair features. She poked at the soil with the toe of her sneaker.

"Yes, really. You started first." Mandy was shy again.

Joel stood up and left them to it. He wandered off to buy another drink.

"I wanted to say I'm really sorry about the squirrel trap."

"It wasn't your fault," Mandy told her. "In fact, you saved his life. And Lauren fixed his broken leg, so everything worked out fine."

Courtney didn't look so sure. "And I'm sorry about ignoring you," she went on. "Only my dad gets sore about stuff like that — you know, things like squirrels and raccoons. And when he's mad, it's best not to hassle him, or else he gets worse. If I'd come over to Pelican's Roost and made friends with you, things might have gotten out of control."

Mandy nodded. "Are you scared of him?" The question slipped out.

"Not scared exactly. With Daddy, you do things his way. It's easier. That's why Joel never admitted he liked animals, too."

Courtney's voice had dropped so low that Mandy could hardly hear what she said. "Will he get mad when he finds out *we*'re friends now?"

"I guess." Courtney fumbled with the straw in her glass of soda.

"Will you tell him?"

Courtney shook her head. "He wouldn't understand."

"Doesn't he even know that you set the squirrel free?"

"No way!" She looked horrified. "Don't tell him, please!"

Mandy promised. But she did want to set things straight as far as she could. "Can I tell my grandma?" she asked.

Reluctantly, Courtney nodded and stood up.

How wrong can you be? Joel had asked.

Even wronger, was the answer. Far from being the spoiled rich kid without a care in the world, Mandy was beginning to see that Courtney had big problems.

"Mr. Miller sounds as if he's a real bully!" she whispered to Joel when he came sauntering back. Courtney had wandered off for a close look at the monkeys.

"That's for sure." They stood watching her from behind.

Suddenly it struck Mandy that Courtney Miller was lonely and scared. "Swimming pool or no swimming pool, dance studio or not, I'd hate to have a dad like that!" she said.

When Mandy got back to Pelican's Roost and repeated the story, Grandma Hope went straight next door to apologize to Courtney. "If I've learned one thing through this, it's never to jump to conclusions!" she declared.

"It must run in the family." Grandpa Hope grinned, as Mandy ran to follow her grandmother. "I take it the tact-and-diplomacy method worked out okay," he shouted after her.

"Terrific!" Mandy called back. "Come on, Joel, bring your swimming things! Mr. Miller's at work and Courtney's invited us both to supper!"

They met up with Courtney by the pool. Now nothing could stop them from laughing and chatting and having a good time — Mandy and Courtney and Joel, all three together. Even Joel forgot to put up a cool front, glad that he could relax with both girls at last.

When Mrs. Miller came onto the lawn to call them in to supper, it was as if they'd known one another for ages.

"What kind of pizza, Mandy?" Courtney served big slices from the sizzling dish. "Four-cheeses, mushroom and tomato, or pepperoni?"

"Mushroom, please." She held out her plate.

"Careful," Mrs. Miller warned as the lavish pizza topping slipped. She was a tall, blond woman with not a hair out of place, dressed in a cool white top and shorts. She fussed over the salads as her daughter handed out slices of pizza.

Mandy was hungry. She piled the delicious food onto her plate, then glanced around at her surroundings. The dining room at Moonshadow had big sliding windows that overlooked the beach. The leaves of the tall palm trees swayed gently in the breeze, and there was a tinge of pink dusk in the sky.

"Did you all have a good day?" Mrs. Miller asked.

They each rushed to tell her the best parts: holding the baby alligator, watching gorillas, setting Allie free.

"Courtney *loves* animals!" her mother gushed. "Just about any kind. Why, her room in Chicago is full of pictures of horses, cats, dogs . . . !"

Mandy grinned at Joel. Now there was no reason for him to pretend not to be interested. "Mine, too," she told them. "I want to be a vet, like my mom and dad."

"Courtney longed to work with animals when she was younger, but now she's changed her mind," Louise Miller explained, as if Courtney couldn't speak for herself. Mandy saw her new friend blush. "Our idea is for her to go to dance school next year, if she works really hard."

"I already do, Mom."

"Sure, honey. Don't make faces. You know your mommy and daddy only want the best for you."

Courtney fiddled with her food. "I wish you'd ask me first," she muttered under her breath. "It's my life." She stood up and turned to Joel and Mandy. "Do you want to see the room where I work out?"

They thanked Mrs. Miller for supper and followed Courtney upstairs. Her studio was a long, empty room with a big mirror lining one wall. In a corner was a large music system.

"Don't you want to go to dance school?" Joel asked. He examined the decks and speakers on the expensive stereo.

"Sure." She sounded bored and listless, then drifted out onto the balcony and looked out to sea. "Well, no, I guess not. But around here it's usually best to do things Daddy's way. Did you hear that?" she asked Mandy, deliberately changing the subject.

"No. What?" Mandy joined her.

"The noise on the roof just then. I think it's those raccoons back again."

"On *your* roof?" Mandy swung around to look.

Joel heard the surprise in her voice and came outside. "Who said anything about raccoons?"

"I did. Mandy probably thinks she's the only one who hears them, but she isn't." Courtney grinned, flicking her hair back. "They're up there most evenings, stomping around like crazy."

"Where?" Mandy listened hard. Then she thought she did hear the familiar scratching and scrabbling.

"You can't see them yet. They don't come down till after dark. Then they run right down, along this balcony."

"How many?" Mandy asked.

"Two. A mother and baby. The same ones you feed."

"You know about that?" Mandy had thought it was a secret between her, Joel, Rita, and Ricky.

"Sure. I give them a little something to eat, then I watch them scoot along our balcony, across our lawn and into the run between your garden and mine. But they don't use the run. They cut out on the other side, into Mr. Logan's garden, and up over the porch onto your roof. You can see clear as anything when the moon shines!"

"Did you say you feed Rita and Ricky?" Mandy spoke more loudly than she'd intended.

Courtney put a finger to her lips. "Ssshh!"

"I didn't know that!" Joel tried to catch up with what

was going on under his own nose. "Have you told your dad?"

"Oh, sure, like I'd go and tell him!" Courtney said scornfully. "*Daddy, we have a couple of raccoons on our roof right now!* He'd love that!"

"What would he do?" Mandy didn't need to ask. She knew the answer before Courtney gave it.

"You heard what he's like. He hates them. But what you don't know is that once my father gets something into his head, nothing's going to shake it out again."

"So if he heard that Rita and Ricky were on his roof, he'd want to kill them?" Joel asked. "I did try and tell you," he told Mandy, reminding her that what she'd taken as a threat had in fact been a warning.

Courtney sighed. "He'd probably pick up the phone and call one of those environmental agencies. There'd be a pest control man here at Moonshadow first thing the next morning!"

Eight

"What we have to do is make the raccoons use a different run!" Mandy outlined a plan. She, Courtney, and Joel had thought long and hard, and come up at last with a way of avoiding trouble for Rita and Ricky.

"Okay, so now that we know that the one between our gardens is too dangerous for them to go on using, it's up to us to persuade them to set up a new run." Joel was sure that this was the right decision. It would only take Mr. Miller to spot the raccoons once for him to bring in pest control.

"No more scampering about on the roof of Pelican's

Roost, no more midnight feasts for Rita and Ricky," Courtney sighed.

As the day turned to dusk, they had to work fast to put their plan into action. They went to Jerry Logan and asked for wooden posts, wire netting, nails, and a hammer.

"We're going to hammer the posts into the ground near the entrance to the raccoon run," Mandy explained. "Then we'll stretch the wire netting across."

"Raccoons are pretty good climbers," Jerry warned. "This'll stop turtles and otters, but it'll need to be a higher fence to keep out Rita and Ricky!"

They decided to try their best anyway, building high fences at each end of the raccoons' favorite route through the garden. But they knew they would have to be cleverer than this for the diversion plan to succeed.

"Mr. Logan's right," Courtney confessed, standing back to examine their work. "It won't take them long to figure out a way around this."

"No, but it might put them off for a while." Mandy paused for breath. "Listen, why don't we use a kind of bait to tempt them to set up a new run?"

"Like what?" Joel gave the idea the thumbs-up. "Like cookies?"

"Yes. And dried fruit. They love that." Mandy noticed

a light come on in Courtney's studio on the first floor at Moonshadow. She stepped quickly out of sight. "I think it's your dad!" she warned.

The others hid in the bushes with her. "Did he see us?" Joel asked.

Courtney kept quiet. She bit her lip and shut her eyes.

"Courtney!" Robert Miller's voice called. He leaned out over the balcony and peered into the dusk. "Who's that hammering out there?"

"He's coming down!" Joel peered out from behind the bush. "He's heading this way."

"Quick, stop him!" Mandy urged. "Don't let him see the run!"

So Courtney ran to the fence and waved. "Hi, Dad. I didn't hear you call!" She sounded falsely cheerful, but nervous at the same time. "You lay the bait to tempt the raccoons away from here," she whispered to Mandy and Joel. "I'll go and throw him off the scent." She slipped through a gap in the fence and ran to meet her father.

"Let's hope she can do it," said Mandy. She waited until the coast was clear. Then she and Joel slipped back into the house. The TV was on in the living room, and the hum of quiet conversation drifted in from the porch. All the grown-ups were settling in for a comfortable evening.

"We've got two problems," Joel pointed out, raiding his grandma's cookie jar for bait. "One is putting this food out where we know it's safe for the raccoons to go. The other is what we do if Mr. Miller finds out!" He spoke fast, stuffing cookies into his pockets and creeping out of the kitchen like a spy.

"Let's deal with the first thing," Mandy decided.

Outside in the garden once more, night had fallen. It wouldn't be long before Rita and Ricky would be leaving the roof at Moonshadow and cutting across the garden to visit Pelican's Roost. Soon, too, other nightly visitors would be ambling along, only to find their usual route to the sea blocked. "How about laying a trail by this opposite fence here?" Mandy pointed to the far side of the garden, well away from Moonshadow. "If the raccoons make a new run here, that should work!"

So they crumbled cookies and laid them under the bushes by the old, unpainted wooden fence that Jerry Logan had built when they'd first moved into the house.

"There's plenty of cover," Joel grunted, crawling on all fours and shifting branches and leaves to clear a tunnel through to the beach. "You know something, Mandy, I think this is going to work!"

"You could be right." But still she thought of all the things that could go wrong. "I just hope all the bait doesn't get eaten up before the raccoons come!"

"Don't think about it!" He stood up at last, brushing the twigs and leaves from his T-shirt. "Will you wake me up and tell me when Rita and Ricky drop by?" he asked shyly.

Mandy promised. Looking around in the gloom, she decided they'd done all they could. "I'll put plenty of fruit out on the porch. We can be pretty sure they'll pay us a visit, can't we?" She needed Joel to reassure her that the plan would work.

"Sure. So should we use these last cookies to make a trail from the porch over to the new run?" He began to lay a thin trickle of crumbs across the garden toward the house.

"Yes — and even if it doesn't work tonight, we can try again tomorrow, and the next night." Mandy was determined to make it happen. Before the end of this vacation, the raccoons would have a safe new run.

Inside the house someone answered the ringing phone. A door opened and a shaft of yellow light fell across the porch. "Joel, Mandy!" Bee Logan called. "It's Courtney for you!"

"Come on!" Joel was off like a shot. He ran ahead into the kitchen and took the phone. "How did you make out?" His dark eyes shone, his hair was messed up, and he was breathing heavily.

Mandy stood by nervously. She tried to read his expression. What was Courtney telling him?

"Did she throw her dad off the track?" she asked as he put down the phone and stared at her. "He didn't find out about the run, did he?"

Joel breathed out and sagged forward. "Nope."

"Thank goodness!"

"Wait. He doesn't know about the run, but he did just hear the raccoons up on the roof at Moonshadow," he reported.

"Oh, no!" Their sharp claws made a loud scuttling noise that could easily be heard from inside Courtney's studio. And Mr. Miller had come out onto the balcony through that room! "What did he do?"

"That's what Courtney called to tell us. He heard the raccoons up on the roof and he told Mrs. Miller. She panicked. Mr. Miller blamed Courtney."

"What for? It wasn't her fault that they were up on the roof!" Mandy pictured the angry scene.

Joel shrugged. "He went crazy, said what does he pay taxes for if it isn't to get rid of vermin?"

"Raccoons aren't vermin!" She was angry herself, almost speechless.

Joel held up his hand. "Courtney says she tried to tell him, but he wouldn't listen. He picked up the phone and dialed a company called Verkil, told them he's overrun by raccoons. He asked them to bring traps and poison."

"What did they say?" Mandy held her breath. Inside, she felt she would explode.

"The man from Verkil took down the Millers' address and said they'd be here first thing tomorrow morning!"

"Raccoons are smart, but they're not *that* smart!" Joel pointed out to Mandy that Rita and Ricky couldn't possibly guess what Robert Miller had in mind for them.

It was the middle of the night and she'd called him, as promised, when the creatures' footsteps woke her.

"I never thought I'd say this," she whispered, "but I really, really wished that Rita and Ricky wouldn't come back!"

There they were, up on the Logans' roof as usual. Joel and Mandy stood barefoot in the garden, hurriedly dressed in shorts and T-shirts, looking up at the two furry faces. Rita checked things out for her young one. She sniffed the air and listened carefully, swishing her striped tail. Baby Ricky ran along the gutter, swung onto the drainpipe, and began to scramble down to ground level.

"You were out of luck. Here they come," Joel whispered, keeping still, fascinated by the baby's movements. "Like I say, they can figure out who their friends

are and where they can find food, but even they can't see into the future. They never heard of pest control, remember!"

"I know," Mandy sighed. Rita and Ricky had followed the usual nighttime track; down from Courtney's roof, across the two gardens, and up onto the roof at Pelican's Roost. Now they were scuttling around on the porch, looking in vain for fruit and water. "But those people are going to come and set traps first thing in the morning!"

"Okay, but don't give up." Joel set off across the garden toward the Millers' house. "Let's see if they got the message about not using the old run!"

Mandy left Rita and Ricky sniffing around the porch and followed him. At least they'd built the fence nice and strong. With luck, the raccoons would have taken that particular hint.

But no. When Joel and Mandy reached the run, they found the wire netting torn away from the sturdy posts and the carefully hammered stakes ripped out of the earth.

"Wow!" Joel gasped. "Who did this?"

"Raccoons. Look!" Mandy pointed to where the soil was deeply scored by sharp claws and to scuffed footprints in the soft earth. "They must be really strong!"

He shrugged. "A great idea, huh?"

"Well, we tried." She sighed and looked back at the house. "The problem is, they like this run and they know every inch of it. It looks like it would take more than a few posts and a bit of wire to stop them from using it."

"Okay, so now we have to carry on with plan two," Joel insisted. If the raccoons wanted to be stubborn, so could he. "Come on, we'll make them an offer they can't refuse!"

"I'm glad you're on my side, at last!" Mandy made a joke of his earlier sulks.

"Yeah, sorry about that." He blushed. "I felt caught in the middle when I thought you and Courtney — kind of, well, you know —"

"Hated each other?" suggested Mandy, smiling. It was good to be over those misunderstandings, too, and working together.

"Come on!" Joel hurried her toward the house.

"Are Ricky and Rita still up there?" Mandy asked, following close on his heels.

"Sure thing." He dug his hands in his pockets and drew out pieces of broken cookies.

"And getting angry, by the look of things." She grinned in spite of everything. Rita was looking everywhere for the food with a look on her face that demanded, "So! Where is it?" She searched under cane chairs, up on the table, and along the windowsill, while Ricky perched hopefully on the balcony rail. "Lay the cookies out this way," Mandy told Joel. "Join them up with the trail we made earlier."

The idea was to lead the raccoons toward the new run. But it didn't take long to realize that she'd spoken too soon.

"Which trail?" Joel felt around in the grass. "Wasn't it right here?"

Mandy nodded. She held out pieces of cookie to tempt Rita and Ricky off the porch.

"Not anymore," he reported. "There's not a single crumb left!"

"You mean, someone ate it already?" Mandy felt her heart sink. So far none of their plans to save the raccoons was working out.

"It looks like it. Maybe squirrels?" Joel peered up into the dark trees. "It really doesn't matter now. What matters is there's nothing left."

It was Mandy's turn to grit her teeth. "Okay, so we lay a fresh trail," she insisted, scattering crumbs toward the far fence. "Come on, Rita, come this way, where it's safe!"

They crouched patiently in the shadows, listening to night birds calling and to the sound of the waves on the shore. At last the waiting paid off. Rita hopped down from the porch and snatched at a piece of cookie. Her head jerked this way and that, looking for danger, then she waited for her baby to join her. Soon they were both picking crumbs from the grass with nimble fingers, steadily following the trail away from the house.

"We did it!" Joel breathed.

Mandy stood up and eased her stiff legs. "It looks like it!" She watched the two raccoons as they worked their way toward the cover of new bushes. They were so busy gobbling the food, she noticed that they'd turned their backs. Their compact, silver-gray bodies were hunched forward, their striped tails raised high.

So Mandy and Joel left them to it, hopeful now that Rita and Ricky would be the first to discover a new run down to the beach, and that others would soon follow their path of beaten-back undergrowth. By the morning, the old and dangerous run down the side of Moonshadow would be deserted.

Mandy went back to bed in good spirits. "When shall we tell Courtney?" she asked Joel as they went their separate ways into their rooms.

"You'd better stay here because of Mr. Miller," he reminded her. "But I'll run over there before breakfast." He gave a wide yawn. "After I get some sleep!"

She smiled and nodded. "Okay, sleep well!" She, too, could hardly wait to crawl back in between the sheets.

But, though she was exhausted and the house was silent, with the nearby waves to lull her, she found she couldn't drift off. She closed her eyes, then jerked them open at the least creak of the old wooden boards or whisper of wind. She turned from one side to the other. Her legs tingled and itched, and her neck grew stiff. Still she lay awake.

It was as if she was waiting. She didn't know what for, but she was expecting — even dreading — something. The clock on the far wall ticked. The moon cast its sharp shadow.

Mandy sat bolt upright. That was it: the noise she'd been straining to hear. She swung her legs over the side of the bed, ready to leap into action. But then she stopped. After all, what could she do?

Her door opened and Joel's head appeared. "Did you hear that?" he whispered.

She tilted her head and stared up at the sloping ceiling. "Yes," she said softly.

There it was again; the sharp, dry sound of feet scuttling across the roof. More than one set; one lighter than the other. It was unmistakable.

"It's them," Joel sighed.

She listened again, refusing to believe it at first, but deep down knowing he was right. The footsteps on the roof were too familiar to deny. "They're back," she agreed, her voice flat and dead. "It's Ricky and Rita."

Her hopes crashed as she realized that their plan had failed.

"Raccoons aren't smart at all!" Courtney cried when she heard the bad news. She'd hurried over to Pelican's Roost early next morning, to tell Mandy and Joel that the men from Verkil had already arrived.

Bee Logan put a bottle of maple syrup and a plate of

pancakes on the kitchen table. "Eat them hot," she encouraged. Back at the stove, she made Jerry Logan and Mandy's grandpa a breakfast of grits and bacon. "And don't let your grandma hear you were up half the night!" she warned Mandy. The bacon sizzled in the pan, mingling with the smell of fresh coffee.

"It's not that they're not clever," Mandy insisted. "But how could any animal know about traps and poison?"

"It takes humans to think up rotten stuff like that," Joel agreed. They sat around the table with solemn faces.

"I asked Daddy over and over not to do this." Courtney had her hair pulled into a ponytail. It made her look younger. Her slight figure was huddled inside a zip-up sweatshirt and sweatpants. "I tried to tell him that raccoons don't mean any harm, but he wouldn't listen, even for a second!" She told them that the men were out there now setting traps on the ground and baiting them.

"How many traps?" Mandy asked.

Courtney shrugged. "Five or six, I guess. These guys come back every morning to see if they . . . have caught anything!"

Her hesitation gave them a chance to picture what would happen: an animal smelling the bait, creeping toward the trap, then *click*! A lever would send its steel jaws crashing down onto the innocent victim. A broken leg at the very least; perhaps a slow bleeding to death.

Mandy shuddered.

"It feels like it's my fault!" Courtney cried.

"No." Joel wouldn't agree. "It's not you, it's your father."

"But it's me in a way. If my family hadn't built Moon-shadow next door and come to live here, this wouldn't be happening!"

Mandy managed to smile and shake her head. "Joel's right." She looked up as Jerry Logan came downstairs. "How good are the traps they're using next door?" she asked him.

He grimaced and went to look out of the window, surprised that work had begun so early. "Pretty good. I'd be lying to you if I told you they weren't," he admitted. "Ask Bee."

"I've seen the results." Bee came with more plates piled high with food. "At GRROWL we get to take care of some of the poor raccoons that survive the traps. Folks bring them in with awful injuries; so bad sometimes that we have to put them to sleep right away. Broken limbs, terrible wounds, and almost always they've lost a lot of blood." She shook her head. "We try to help, but it's often too late."

"Yes, but anyhow you try," Jerry put in. "And you're the only place that does!" He explained that no other rescue centers in the state even considered taking in injured raccoons.

"Are you saying that it's only a matter of time before these traps catch Ricky and Rita?" Mandy asked. Going to join Jerry Logan at the window, she caught sight of two men at work. They were bending over to disguise the metal frame of one of their contraptions with grass and leaves. In the background she could see the stern figure of Courtney's dad looking on.

"Yes, you have a problem," he admitted. "This garden here at Pelican's Roost is a fine place for wildlife, and your raccoons, your otters, and your turtles — they all know it. They come and go as they please. Sooner or later, they're going to come rooting around that old run and then they're going to pick up a tasty scent from one of those traps!" He turned away and went to eat his breakfast. "Looks to me like there isn't a thing we can do to stop it," he said.

It was low tide at twelve, midday. Mandy, Courtney, and Joel stood on the beach. The sun blazed down on their backs, the sand was hot underfoot. They watched five raccoons washing clam shells at the water's edge and scooping out the contents.

"Any other day we'd think this was great," Joel muttered.

"Not today." Mandy looked beyond the raccoons to the clumsy pelicans bobbing in the shallow waves. Everything was so peaceful, so quiet.

"What are we going to do?" Courtney pleaded. All morning they'd secretly manned the fence where the traps were set, shooing away any creature that ventured near. "We can't keep a lookout forever!"

"No. We'd need to be in half a dozen places at once," Mandy admitted. She'd spotted Rita and Ricky among the bunch on the shore.

Just then a cruiser cut across the open sea, heading toward the harbor at Blue Bayous. The noise disturbed the feeding raccoons. They looked up jerkily and threw down the shells, fussing and scattering as the boat drew near. Two shot off along the shore, two toward the grounds at Pelican's Roost, but Rita and Ricky headed straight for Moonshadow.

They ran blindly, frightened by the engine's roar. For a moment, Mandy and the others stood by helplessly.

"Quick, we've got to get there first!" Mandy began to run through the loose, dry sand. She sank ankle-deep, a clumsy, slow figure. Meanwhile, the agile little animals had gained some distance on her. While Mandy tried hard to get clear of the sand, Joel and Courtney saw Rita and Ricky disappear into the bushes. Instinct had taken them to the thick undergrowth by the stream that trickled down from Moonshadow.

"It's no good, they're too fast!" Joel saw them vanish in the shadows with a backward glance and a flash of their white faces.

But Mandy, Joel, and Courtney ran on anyway, only slowing down when they came to the bushes. They splashed into the clear water, heading upstream after the raccoons, bending low under the overhanging branches, and stumbling over wet, slippery rocks.

"Wait!" Mandy said, catching up with her friends and holding up her hand to listen. An unseen bird spread its wings and clattered out of the bush up ahead. Then there was silence. She was angry with herself for having wasted precious seconds. "No, it was nothing. Let's go!"

They waded on until they reached the boundaries of the Millers' garden: a clean white fence, and a sign warning beachcombers that this was private land. Still, there was no sign, no sound of Rita and Ricky.

"Maybe they took a different route!" Courtney gasped, panting.

They stood to listen again. There was just enough time to hear the drowsy midday silence, to hope that she was right. Suddenly a loud squeal split the air. It was the cry of an animal in pain!

Mandy almost doubled over with shock. It was as if she'd been shot. The squeal tore through all of them, high and terrified. There was a crashing sound in the undergrowth; a second animal retreating in panic.

Mandy forced herself forward, letting the branches scratch and catch at her clothes as she blundered on. Even now, she refused to believe that it had happened.

"Mandy, come back!" Joel yelled. "We don't know where they set those traps!" He warned her not to stumble into one as she rushed forward out of sight.

She didn't care. All she could hear was the shrill, piercing cry. She followed the sound, dreading what she would find.

Nine

It was Ricky who was caught in the trap.

Mandy found him screaming with pain, his front paw clamped inside the metal jaws.

Across the wide, smooth lawn, a door in the house opened and Louise Miller came rushing out.

From the bush beside the trap, Rita emerged. She darted toward her screaming baby, begging him to pick himself up and follow her.

"He can't, Rita!" Mandy shook her head. The sight of the desperate mother roused her. "His leg's trapped!" She searched for something that could pry apart the vicious hinge that held the trap in place.

Joel arrived, took in the scene at once, and picked up a large, smooth stone. "Use this!" he urged. "Jam it right in!"

Still Rita darted toward the trap, begging Ricky to follow her.

"Oh, no!" Mrs. Miller ran across the lawn, hands to her cheeks, her face pale. "It's only a baby. Oh, Courtney, honey, I never realized . . . What shall we do?"

Too late to think of that now! Mandy said to herself as she shoved the stone into the hinge. By this time, terror had overcome Ricky and the screaming had stopped. He stared blank-eyed as Mandy tried to free him. Rita, too, had given up trying to encourage him. She climbed into the bush and stared down, watching Mandy's every move.

"Hurry up!" Courtney pleaded, on her hands and knees beside the wounded animal. "His leg's bleeding!"

"Yes, and this trap's strong," said Mandy through gritted teeth. She shoved with all her might, and felt the trap ease a fraction. Then she stepped onto the lower arm of the hinge and began to tug at the upper section. "Come on!" she muttered time and again. It took everything she had to pry it apart.

"Careful it doesn't snap shut!" Mrs. Miller hovered uselessly at the edge of the group, peering through her fingers, unable to look.

Eventually, Mandy thought she could just ease Ricky

out. She stooped and gently pulled him clear. As she lifted him and stepped back, the shift of weight made the trap do exactly what Louise Miller had warned them about. It sprang shut with a loud snap.

Mandy jumped. In her fright, she let Ricky escape from between her hands. He dropped to the ground and rolled over. In a flash, Rita leaped from the bush. She scooped him up, made him cling to the long fur of her belly, and supported him with one arm. Then she whisked around, carrying him clumsily, making off across the lawn.

"Don't let her get away!" Mandy cried. "Stop her. If we don't get Ricky to the Rescue Center, he'll bleed to death!"

But no one could stop the mother raccoon. All she knew was that she had her injured baby safe in her arms. Something dreadful and unexpected had happened to him to make him cry out in pain, but now he was free. She would look after him!

She ran faster than Mandy and the others, reached the smooth patio beside the Millers' swimming pool, looked frantically here and there for the safety of bushes, undergrowth, or trees. There was none to be had in the Millers' perfect, manicured garden. So Rita made the only choice left open to her. With Ricky still clinging precariously to her, she ran toward the house.

"Stop her!" Courtney pleaded.

Rita launched herself at the tall mosquito screen across the front porch. She clambered up it with Ricky, reached the top, then scrambled onto the sloping roof out of reach. Up she climbed to the highest point on Moonshadow's immense roof.

Safe! Only then did she stop and look back down into the garden at the anxious faces staring up at her and her badly injured baby.

"Wait here. Your father's at work. I'll call him!" Louise Miller was the first to move. She told Courtney to keep an eye on the two raccoons.

"No, don't do that!" cried Courtney. She saw what would happen. "He'll be mad. He won't want to help us get them down!"

"That's silly, honey! He has to know. I'll tell him that one is only a poor little baby!" Mrs. Miller gave a determined nod and vanished into the house.

But Mandy and Joel agreed they had to move fast to get Rita and Ricky down off the roof before Robert Miller had time to act. They didn't trust his reaction and Mandy was worried about Ricky's wound.

"He's already lost a lot of blood," she told them. "He's pretty weak, and he's in shock. I don't think we can afford to wait!"

"So what's the plan?" Joel wanted to know.

"You go and tell Bee what's happened," Mandy decided. "Ask her to stand by, ready to take Ricky to the Rescue Center as soon as we get him down from the roof!"

Joel sped off across the lawn. He vaulted the white fence and made straight for Pelican's Roost, yelling for help at the top of his voice.

Meanwhile, Mandy tried to work out the best way to climb up onto the roof.

"Let *me* go!" Courtney pleaded. She hauled herself up on to the rail that ran the length of the porch. "It's my house. I want to go up there!"

"Wait, we don't want to scare Rita away!" Mandy knew that the raccoon would soon take fright. She followed Courtney and swung herself up onto the first low roof. Beyond and above this there was the main roof of the house, and it was up onto this that they would have to climb next.

"No, I can do this!" Courtney reached up and gripped a drainpipe. She would have to climb about three yards to come level with the edge of the roof.

"We'll both go," Mandy decided. After all, she was the one who knew Rita, the one who'd been her friend. "If she sees me, maybe she'll know we're only trying to help!"

She followed Courtney, finding footholds on the

brackets that held the pipe to the wall, hoping and praying that they could get to Ricky in time.

"Okay, now we have to creep up slowly," Courtney whispered. She was on the roof at last, waiting for Mandy. "They're still here. Rita looks pretty scared. She's watching our every move!"

Mandy joined her. She tried not to look down, knowing that the height would make her dizzy. It took a while to get her balance on the slope, then she felt in her pocket for leftover cookies that might tempt Rita to come toward them. But when she looked up at the mother raccoon, squatting on the ridge of the roof, eyeing them with fear, she realized that a treat would be no good. She began to talk gently instead, inching her way toward her.

"That's right, it's me," she whispered. "You know who I am, don't you? I'm your friend!"

Rita shivered, holding Ricky close to her chest. She shifted away to one side as Mandy and Courtney made their way up the long slope toward her.

Mandy paused and held up her hand. "She's so frightened I don't think she recognizes me," she warned.

Courtney nodded. She balanced by holding out both arms, wobbling slightly. "Let's split up," she suggested. "You go straight ahead, while I work my way around the side and come up from behind."

Taking a deep breath and forgetting for a second not to look down, Mandy saw the ground spin beneath them. She saw Joel running back through the garden at Pelican's Roost, and Bee Logan and Grandpa following more slowly. Help was coming, at least. "Okay," she whispered, regaining her balance as she looked up once more.

They began to edge toward the frightened raccoon. Mandy could see Ricky crouching in his mother's arm, his front leg bleeding. Time was running out for him, she knew. They must make a big effort, rush the last few yards over the roof, and take Rita by surprise. "Ready?" she whispered to Courtney, who had worked her way around the back as planned.

Courtney nodded. She steadied herself, waiting for Mandy to give the order.

"Let's go!" Mandy pushed herself up the slope, ready to reach out and take hold of both the mother and baby. But the sudden movement was too much for Rita. She jerked away, losing hold of Ricky as she did so. The baby raccoon slid out of her arms and down the roof toward Mandy, who put out her hands to stop him.

Courtney saw it happen. She screamed, reached out at the same time, made a grab for Rita, and missed.

Mandy lunged to catch hold of Ricky as he tumbled, and felt his soft fur between her hands.

But Courtney clutched at thin air. She lost her balance and began to slide. While Rita slid out of her grasp, Courtney fell forward onto the roof and slithered down — past Mandy and Ricky, down toward the edge of the roof.

From the garden Joel yelled a warning. Mrs. Miller ran out of the house, fresh from her phone call. She looked up to see her daughter sliding down the roof, then clinging to the gutter by her fingertips, her legs dangling.

"Oh, no!" Louise Miller stood paralyzed with fear.

"Hang on!" Grandpa Hope came running across the garden.

Mandy watched from above. The sliding, slipping, scraping sound stopped. There was silence.

Mandy clutched Ricky fearfully. Everyone gazed up helplessly as Courtney's grip weakened. Her fingers lost their hold. She screamed once more, then fell.

Ten

In the silence that followed Courtney's fall, Mandy slithered down the roof with Ricky. The little raccoon lay still in her arms, making no attempt to follow his mother, who had fled to the far side of the roof, out of sight.

"I'll take him!" Joel urged as she reached the edge. He stretched out his arms, standing on the porch rail, while the grown-ups ran to help Courtney.

Mandy handed over the injured baby, then eased herself down to ground level. All around was chaos.

Louise Miller crouched over Courtney's unconscious figure, crying and pleading for her to wake up. Grandpa Hope ran to the phone.

Bee Logan gave instructions. "Don't move her! She might have broken bones. Okay, let me check to see what her breathing's like."

Joel was silent as he handed Ricky back to Mandy. He knew there was nothing they could do for him until they'd found out about Courtney. His face was white and tense as they crept forward to look.

Bee leaned close to Courtney, putting her cheek against her mouth. "She's breathing!" Then she checked her pulse. "We need to get her to the hospital. Call an ambulance!"

Grandpa reappeared. "It's on its way."

At that moment, a large black car appeared in the drive. It crunched over the gravel and stopped with a skid of its wheels. Robert Miller jumped out.

"What's going on?" He'd been called back from work by his wife to deal with a raccoon caught in one of the traps. Instead, he found his daughter lying unconscious. He ran quickly to her side.

"Oh, Robert, it's all my fault!" Louise Miller cried. "Courtney didn't want us to set those traps. Now look!" Tears streamed down her face as she stroked her daughter's cheek.

"Never mind that now." Courtney's father fell onto his knees beside her. "Just tell me what happened!"

Gently, Bee Logan explained. She told him that the

paramedics were coming. "I can't say for sure, but I think she's broken her leg." She pointed to the one that lay bent awkwardly under the girl's body.

"Oh!" Louise Miller sobbed. "We've done this!"

"Hush." Mr. Miller was shocked into silence to see his daughter like this. For once in his life, he didn't want to have the last word.

"But, Robert, this is Courtney's whole future! You know what a broken leg could mean to her career!"

"We can't think of that right now. Why did she climb up there in the first place?" Robert Miller needed to know. "What possessed her?" He looked around the group for an explanation.

"She wanted to save Ricky before you got here." Mandy stepped forward, holding the raccoon. It was the only sentence she could think of to say. It came out before she had a chance to consider its effect.

"Great, so it's my fault!" Mr. Miller gritted his teeth and looked down at Courtney.

"She's coming around!" Grandpa Hope warned them not to argue as the girl's eyelids flickered and she moved her head. Slowly her gray eyes opened.

And then the ambulance came wailing up the quiet road, lights flashing, siren sounding. It swung into the drive. Soon two paramedics were running toward them with a stretcher and splints.

It was out of their hands now. The experts worked quickly, assessing the situation and moving Courtney with great care onto the stretcher. They took over, telling the Millers to travel to the hospital with them, and sliding the stretcher into the ambulance. Within a couple of minutes, doors were slamming, and wheels were crunching away up the drive. Bee, Grandpa Hope, Mandy, and Joel were left standing in silence.

"Will we be in time?" Mandy urged Bee Logan to drive faster. They were making their own emergency dash to the hospital; for Ricky, not Courtney.

As soon as the ambulance had gone, they'd snapped into action, running next door with the injured raccoon, jumping into Jerry's truck, and leaving instructions with Grandpa Hope to let the others know what was going on. Mandy and Joel drove with Bee to GRROWL.

The truck bumped along the rough trail leading through the wildlife sanctuary, raising pale dust and making the flocks of pink spoonbills rise from the lake and fly to a safe distance. Mandy glanced down at Ricky. She'd wrapped up the injured paw with one of her grandpa's handkerchiefs, torn into strips and bound tightly around his leg. It had helped stop the bleeding, but the poor creature was weak and confused. "Can't we go any faster?" she pleaded.

"I'm going as fast as this old truck can go!" Bee gripped the steering wheel, and swerved to avoid a pothole in the road. They skidded sideways, then righted themselves.

Mandy hung on with one hand, cradling Ricky with the other. She thought about poor Rita, left stranded on the roof at Moonshadow. She'd been looking down at them as they ran with her baby, running up and down the slope in sudden, terrified darts, helpless as they took Ricky away. What would she do now? Where would she go without him?

"Okay, this is it!" Bee Logan pulled up outside the Rescue Center at last. Duchess, the Great Dane, came bounding down from the first-floor balcony to greet them, and the vet herself soon followed.

"Hi, Bee! I wasn't expecting you, was I?" Her cheerful greeting soon turned brisk and professional when she saw the injured animal. "Okay, bring him up, Mandy. Right into the Intensive Care Unit. He looks in pretty bad shape. Let's get a move on it!"

Mandy ran up the steps. By now, Ricky was so weak that his eyes were beginning to close, and he wasn't reacting to his surroundings. She rushed into the emergency room and laid him on the table.

Quickly Lauren released an oxygen tube from its stand and fixed a mask over the raccoon's nose and mouth. She unwrapped the bandage from his wound, injected a needle into his other leg, then connected the needle to a drip. "He needs fluid to help with the trauma," she explained. Another needle for antibiotics, then an expert examination of the wound.

"How is he?" Mandy hovered at the far side of the table.

"The flesh is badly torn," Lauren told her. "But the bone may be okay. It's blood loss and shock we have to worry about here." She checked Ricky's heartbeat. "Sometimes an accident can literally scare an animal to death!"

"This was no accident," Mandy muttered. She explained about the trap, looking at tiny Ricky stretched out on the table, struggling to survive.

"Okay, I'm going to bandage him up again real good and tight," Lauren decided. "Once we get some fluid into him, he stands a better chance. We're going to keep him warm."

"Will you have to operate on the leg?"

"I can't tell until I've taken an X ray. But that comes later. First, we have to hope that he makes it through the next twenty-four hours."

Lauren worked calmly, asking for Mandy's help to move Ricky into a special unit where he could be monitored.

Gradually, the panic that Mandy had felt when she first heard Ricky scream began to ease. He was in good hands now, she knew. She found time to explain to Lauren what had happened, describing Courtney's fall. "We still don't know if she'll be okay," she told her. "Mrs. Miller was pretty upset, and Mr. Miller was stunned." In fact, she hadn't expected to see him like that; pale and silent as they lifted Courtney into the ambulance.

"Any parent would be," Lauren pointed out.

"I thought he'd be mad at Joel and me."

"People can surprise you during an emergency. Anyhow, at least our patient is doing okay." She nodded at Ricky inside his plastic cage.

"Shall I go and tell Joel and Bee?" Mandy said quietly, satisfied to see Ricky curled up there. He seemed settled and a little calmer.

Lauren nodded. "And thanks, Mandy."

She blushed.

"No, you were great. Without you he wouldn't have stood a chance."

"Thanks." She managed a brief smile. Then she went down to report to the others. "We have to keep our fingers crossed," she told them, feeling suddenly shaky and tired.

Bee Logan looked at her with concern. "Come on,

Mandy, honey, let's get you home!" She ushered her back into the truck. "It's okay, Lauren will call if she has any news!"

Mandy didn't have the energy to protest, so she slid onto the seat and closed her eyes, hearing Joel climb up alongside her.

"What do you think, is Ricky going to be okay?" he wanted to know.

It was the question no one could answer. Mandy opened her eyes and gazed straight ahead as Bee set off down the trail. The truck bumped and rattled away from the Rescue Center. "We'll know tomorrow," she replied, sinking back against the seat.

That evening, Jerry Logan saw Robert and Louise Miller arrive back from the hospital alone.

He came into the kitchen at Pelican's Roost, where everyone had gathered to wait for news. "It looks like they kept Courtney in the hospital," he told them. "That must mean it's pretty bad."

"Well, she was unconscious, after all," Grandma Hope reminded them. "They would have to keep her in for a concussion, wouldn't they?"

Mandy listened to the discussion without playing any part. Somehow it seemed that it hardly had anything to do with her anymore. She was still tired and shivery, even though it was a warm evening.

"Maybe one of us should go and ask how Courtney is?" Bee suggested. "Or maybe give them a call? What do you think?"

They hesitated. No one wanted to upset the Millers even more by doing the wrong thing. On the other hand, they really wanted to know how Courtney was.

"We'll go in person," Grandma decided. "Mandy, shall it be you and me?"

She nodded. It seemed to be a huge effort just to stand up, but she wanted to be one of the ones who went to find out.

"Are you okay?" Joel asked quietly. He'd kept in the background all afternoon, but it was out of worry, not carelessness, she knew.

Mandy nodded and followed her grandma out of the house. Outside in the garden, all was quiet. The sky was turning spectacular shades of pink and gold as dusk came. "Now, if the Millers don't want to talk to us, that would be quite understandable," Grandma Hope warned her. "Especially if the news is bad."

Mandy braced herself as they went and knocked at the door. They waited, knocked again.

"Someone's coming!" Grandma whispered at last.

There were footsteps in the hall, and a light went on

in the porch. Robert Miller opened the door. When he saw who it was, he took a step back.

"No, wait, please!" Grandma stopped him from closing the door on them. "How's Courtney? What did the hospital tell you?"

"Who is it, Robert?"

Mandy heard Louise Miller's high, quavery voice in the background.

"Never mind. I'll deal with it, honey," he told her.

But Mrs. Miller herself appeared in the doorway, her face drained, her eyes red from crying.

"How is she?" Grandma repeated the question, taking a step inside the house, though she hadn't been invited.

Tears flooded Louise Miller's eyes again and Mandy dreaded the answer. But they were tears of relief after anxious hours of waiting at the hospital.

"She has a broken leg," Mrs. Miller told them through her sobs. "But no other bones are broken. And no internal injuries."

"Thank goodness!" Grandma took hold of Mrs. Miller's hand. "And there's nothing else?"

Louise Miller shook her head. "Cuts and bruises. A slight concussion. They've kept her overnight, but as far as they can tell, there's nothing serious!"

Mandy took in the news. "She was lucky!" she breathed.

But Robert Miller gave her a sharp look. "You call a broken leg and concussion lucky?" he retorted, turning away with a scowl.

Mandy's heart sank. Mr. Miller was back to his old, bullying self. He strode across the hallway, snapping the blinds shut and making it clear that he wanted them to go.

"Climbing up onto a roof to get some useless raccoons. You call that lucky?" He turned to glare at Mandy.

She felt his eyes bore a hole through her.

"I call it a foolish thing to do!" He flung his final remark at her, then stormed upstairs.

Eleven

"There's one good thing to come out of all this," Jerry told Mandy as he went around the house that night, putting up mosquito screens and closing windows. "I haven't seen hide nor hair of any raccoons down that old run since your little one got caught in the trap. It sure did scare them off!"

Mandy agreed. Since she'd gotten back from the Millers' house with the good news about Courtney, she and Joel had been out to check. Sure enough, the old run was deserted.

"You know what they say, every cloud has a silver lining."

Mandy helped fix the last screen into place. But she didn't feel like being cheerful, not yet. "Except for Mr. Miller," she reminded him. "He's not going to let this whole thing drop."

"Hang in there. You can never tell what a father will do when his kid gets hurt. It kind of knocks him off balance."

"Apart from that, there's still Rita to worry about," she insisted. "It must look to her like she's lost the thing she cares most about in the whole world!"

The mother raccoon was out there somewhere; in the trees, scuttling along the banks of the stream, or simply standing waiting, all alone. Mandy kept seeing her in her mind's eye.

"Any news from the Center?" Jerry asked, before he went indoors.

"Not yet." Lauren hadn't called about Ricky.

"Hmm. I guess it'll be morning before she calls." Mandy sighed.

"You coming in?" He waited in the doorway, framed in a square of yellow lamplight.

"Soon." She was so tired, yet not sleepy exactly. She stayed out on the porch, listening and waiting.

"Hey." A quiet voice interrupted her thoughts.

"Hey," she said back to Joel without turning around.

"Are you wondering what happened to Rita?" he asked.

"Yep. Are you?"

"I was. But come and take a look." Joel led her inside the house and up the stairs. He took her through her own room, but out onto the balcony. "I heard her up on the roof," he explained, waiting for Mandy to see what he meant.

Her eyes got used to the moonlight after the glow of the lamps indoors. She made out the palm trees in the garden, the shabby wooden rail that ran the length of the balcony. And there, huddled on the rail, with her striped tail drooping, her dark eyes glittering, sat faithful Rita!

Mandy drew a sharp breath. She longed to explain, to tell Rita not to worry; that Ricky was hurt but that he was being well taken care of.

The raccoon stared back at them, shifting slightly on the rail, as if to say, *"Where's my baby? What have you done with him?"*

Mandy could read the questions in every flicker of her staring eyes. "It's okay," she whispered. "We're doing our best. Don't give up!"

But the sound of her voice disturbed the raccoon. Rita stretched out a paw and clung to a nearby post. She swung out of reach, back onto the roof, where they heard her scurry away.

"She doesn't trust us anymore!" Mandy turned and

went inside. "And I don't blame her, not after what's happened today." This was the saddest thing; going to bed at last and listening for Rita's steps, thinking of her on the roof in the moonlight, alone and unhappy.

"Good news!" Bee Logan put down the phone and called Mandy and Joel down from their rooms early the next morning. "That was Lauren. Ricky made it through the night!"

"Great!" Joel's face split into a broad grin.

"What else?" Mandy came down, toothbrush in hand, her mouth full of toothpaste. "What else did she say about him?"

"He had a good night. She just X-rayed the leg this morning and it's like she thought: no bones broken. All he needs are a couple of stitches in the wound and time to get over the shock!" Bee beamed back at them.

"When can we go visit?" Joel wanted to know. He'd flung open the kitchen door and rushed out into the garden to look up onto the roof.

"Lauren said to wait until this afternoon," Bee replied, going back to her stove. "He needs plenty of rest this morning."

Mandy followed Joel out of the house. "What are you doing?"

"You hear that?" he yelled to Rita up on the roof.

"There's no one there!" she protested. "I heard her leave before it got light." She'd been awake for most of the night, worrying and wondering what would happen even if little Ricky survived. Now she went in to talk to Bee about it.

"How long before we know for sure that he's going to be okay?" she asked, sitting down to breakfast. This morning she felt she could eat, so she had eggs and pancakes.

"A few days. Lauren will give him a course of antibiotics to stop any infection. By then the wound should have healed up. Why?"

"What then? Will he have to stay at GRROWL?" Mandy was beginning to think ahead. "Or will he be able to come home?"

Bee tilted her head to one side and kept busy at the stove. She obviously didn't want to commit herself either way. "I guess we'll have to wait and see on that one," she said.

Waiting was one of the things Mandy wasn't good at.

"That's tight enough, Mandy!" Jerry Logan warned. He'd watched her screw the tops onto a row of jars on the kitchen table. She'd been helping Grandma and Bee Logan to make strawberry jam. "If you screw them on any tighter, we'll never get them off again!"

"Sorry, I wasn't thinking."

Her grandma took the jars away and stacked them on a shelf. "Never mind, not long now," she promised. "Once we've had lunch, you can go with Bee to the Center and see how your precious little patient is getting along!"

"Speaking of patients, look who's just come home!" Grandpa Hope called from the porch. He was sitting and rocking in the sun.

Mandy and Joel went out to see Courtney being helped out of her father's car and into a chair by the swimming pool next door. She had one leg splinted and wrapped up, and could only move by leaning on a crutch. Her mother tried to help, but Courtney looked as if she wanted to do it by herself.

"They let her out!" Relief made Joel blow his cheeks out and give a big sigh. "Maybe we should go and visit?" he suggested to Mandy.

Mandy looked at her grandfather. "Perhaps they won't want us to bother them." She remembered how Robert Miller was the night before, and the piercing stare he'd given her. She hoped that her grandpa would say they should delay the visit.

But Grandpa Hope waved away her objection. "Don't be silly. I'm sure they'd like you to stop by."

So Mandy had to follow Joel. He took the shortcut,

through the garden and over the fence, racing to give Courtney the latest news on Ricky.

Robert and Louise Miller were fussing over their daughter, trying to get her to be still and rest by the pool. Mr. Miller was the first to hear their visitors. He looked up with a frown. "Oh, it's you two. Courtney's too tired to see you. Could you come back later?" he began.

But their friend interrupted. "I'm not tired," she protested. "Come and tell me about Ricky."

And, for once, Louise Miller was prepared to override her husband. "Oh, such good news from the hospital!" she cried, standing up and coming to meet them. "The doctors say it's a clean break. It's going to heal really quick!"

"That's great." It was a load off Mandy's mind, too.

"And she'll still be able to dance and work out and all! Of course, she'll have to take it easy at first, but they say there's no reason to think there's any permanent damage. When we think of how much worse it could have been, we're just so grateful!" Mrs. Miller drew Mandy in by the hand. "See for yourself. She looks okay, doesn't she?"

Courtney sat in her white cane chair looking embarrassed. "Mom, I can talk for myself!" Her injured leg stuck out at a right angle; the crutch was propped against a nearby table. "Stupid, huh?" she murmured with a shy grin at Mandy and Joel.

"No, it took guts to go up on that roof!" Joel protested. "You, too, Mandy!"

"Huh!" Robert Miller grunted.

"Don't you encourage them!" Mrs. Miller told Joel, teasing now that she was sure Courtney was going to be fine.

"If you'd had any sense, you'd have let the pest control guys get on with their work and minded your own business," Mr. Miller voiced his opinion. It was clear he hadn't changed his mind.

But Courtney's accident seemed to have given her the courage to stand up to him. "Daddy, if you'd been here and heard the baby raccoon cry out, you wouldn't think that way!" She turned to Mandy and pressed for answers to her questions about Rita and Ricky. "How's Ricky? Did you get him down from the roof?"

Mandy told her everything that had happened since Courtney had knocked herself unconscious. "We hope Ricky's going to be okay. Joel's grandmother is planning to drive us over there this afternoon."

"Oh, can I come?" Courtney's eyes lit up.

"Honey, you know what they said at the hospital. You

have to take it easy," Louise Miller warned, fussing around her daughter like an anxious mother hen.

"But, Mom, I'd like to see little Ricky!" She looked to her father. "Daddy, please!"

Certain that Robert Miller would say no, Mandy signaled at Joel for them to back off. "We'll come and tell you how he is," she murmured.

But Mr. Miller stopped her. "Let me get this straight. Is Ricky the raccoon you risked your neck for?" he asked his daughter.

Courtney nodded, her eyes filling with tears.

"Yes, and he's very special!"

For a moment she tried to lift herself from her chair, then she sat back. Her face glowed with emotion as she defended the young raccoon. "He's smart as anything. You should see him follow a trail of food, just like his mom. Every day he learns something new. And he trusted me, Dad! He and his mom came to our house because they thought we were their friends. Then they went next door; right across the garden and through the fence. You should see them. They're amazing!"

As Courtney spoke up for the raccoons, Mandy felt proud. She said all the things Mandy would have wanted to say, and she gave her father the message loud and clear.

"Huh!" Robert Miller said again. This time, he gave his head a shake. "I never knew that."

"Back home, we think of them as pests," Louise Miller whispered to Mandy. "I guess that's the way most people look at them."

"Who cares about most people?" Courtney tried again to stand up. "Can I go to see Ricky at the Rescue Center?" she pleaded.

Her father held on to her arm, then gave her the crutches. "I never knew any of this!"

"Can I?"

Robert Miller made up his mind. "Okay," he said, to everyone's amazement. "I'll drive you there myself!"

His wife showered him with protests, but Robert Miller wouldn't hear any of them. He told Joel to run and tell Bee Logan that there was no need for her to drive the truck up the island; he would take all three kids to visit the baby raccoon.

"Can you believe it!" Courtney whispered to Mandy as they sat waiting in the backseat of the car. Her father was inside making phone calls, putting off his work appointments.

"He knows he shouldn't have set the traps in the first place," Mandy said.

They didn't have time to discuss it. Soon, Joel had jumped in the front passenger seat, and Robert Miller, who had changed into a blue polo shirt and casual trousers, was starting the car.

He drove smoothly up to GRROWL, following Joel's instructions, saying little. Mandy noticed that he kept glancing in the driver's mirror to check on Courtney. And when they arrived at the Rescue Center, he insisted on lifting her out of the car and setting her down on a chair that Joel ran to get. Then he stood up and took a good look around.

"Hi!" Lauren greeted them from the balcony, while Duchess bounded down the steps to say hello. "I didn't recognize the car."

Mandy introduced her to Mr. Miller. "Courtney's come to see Ricky with us," she explained. "But I'm wondering how we're going to get her up the steps."

"No need." Lauren was relaxed and smiling. "I just took him off the drip and out of intensive care."

"So you can bring him down here?" Joel asked. He was impatient to see Ricky himself.

"Sure." Lauren retraced her steps up to the first floor.

"What a great place!" Courtney whispered. She gazed at the pelicans with injured wings, lame deer, orphan skunks, otters, and raccoons. "I'm really glad we came!" She smiled up at her father.

Then Lauren brought Ricky down and handed him straight to Courtney, with Mandy, Joel, and Robert Miller looking on.

Mandy could see at once that Ricky was over the worst. Instead of the lifeless, trembling little creature with dazed eyes that she'd handed over to Lauren the day before, here was a bright-eyed little raccoon with a bandaged front leg. His fur was soft and clean again, with only a small patch of shaved fur where the injection for the drip had been.

"Poor little Ricky!" Courtney crooned, holding him to her cheek. "We've both got hurt legs! But I'm glad you're going to be okay!"

"No problem," Lauren reassured them. "Ricky will be one of our success stories!"

"When can he come home?" Courtney asked, her eyes filling up with tears of relief.

"In a couple of days, when the stitches have done their job. He's young and healthy. Young ones always stand the best chance of being rehabilitated into the wild." Lauren smiled at Mandy as she spoke, knowing that they were all hanging on her every word. "There's only one problem . . ." She hesitated and turned to Mr. Miller. "It's these traps."

Before she could say another word, Robert Miller jumped in. "I know. It's all my fault. I never knew what it meant to Courtney, believe me!"

Lauren nodded and listened. "They're pretty cruel contraptions," she told him.

"I realize that now. I'm from the city. I don't have much experience with these things."

Mandy risked a sideways glance at Joel. She saw him holding his breath, just like her.

"I understand," Lauren spoke quietly, waiting for him to go on. She kept one eye on Courtney and Ricky, showing her how to hold him without hurting his injured leg.

"But listen, as soon as I get back home, I'm going to get them to come and take those traps away!"

Mr. Miller came out with what they were all longing to hear. Mandy sighed with relief. No more traps. Freedom for the raccoons to come and go as they pleased!

"You mean it?" Courtney looked up at him with shining eyes.

Her father crouched beside her and Ricky. He put out a hand to stroke the raccoon. "Sure, honey. I just hope you can forgive me for setting them in the first place!"

For two days and nights Mandy and Joel heard Rita's lonely footsteps on the roof.

The pest control men came to Moonshadow and took away the cruel traps. Jerry Logan removed the fencing that had blocked the old raccoon run. Soon there were tracks in the soil to show that the turtles, otters, and raccoons had returned.

On Wednesday evening, Robert Miller came over to Pelican's Roost to talk to Bee.

"I'd like to apologize for the trouble I've caused," he began.

Bee didn't bear a grudge. "That's okay. It takes a while to settle into a new neighborhood, find out how things operate."

Mandy and Joel sat cross-legged on the porch, playing a card game.

"And I've been talking with Louise about how we can make it up to you. She said for me to ask Courtney. I did, and Courtney came up with a really good idea." Delving into his jacket pocket, Robert Miller produced a long slip of white paper and laid it flat on the table.

Bee put on her glasses and picked it up. "This is a check for a thousand dollars!"

Jerry peered over her shoulder. "Made out to the Group for the Rescue and Rehabilitation of Wild Life!"

"This is wonderful!" Bee Logan began, her face lighting up. "Oh, wait till I tell Lauren! Think of all the things we can do with a thousand dollars!"

"On top of that, I've been thinking how we can raise the profile of the Rescue Center." Mr. Miller let them know how much he wanted to help. "My idea is that we can put brochures in all my real estate offices, telling people about the work that goes on at GRROWL. That way, we get a lot more volunteers and more donations of money!"

"We hope!" Bee was still beaming. "This is wonderful, Robert! I can't tell you how grateful we are!"

But Mr. Miller didn't wait to be thanked. Instead, he strode off up the garden, blushing to the roots of his fair hair, as Bee Logan's praises rang in everyone's ears.

The next morning, Lauren came to thank the Millers in person. From the bedroom window, Mandy saw her truck drive up to Moonshadow, saw her swing down from the driver's seat, and stride up to the house. Five minutes later, Courtney came hobbling out with the vet. They got into the truck and headed toward Pelican's Roost.

Mandy scooted downstairs. "Hey, Joel, Lauren's here!"

Together they went to meet her.

"Guess who I've got here!" She greeted them with a happy smile and lifted a small cage out of the truck.

"Ricky!" Joel and Mandy chorused.

Courtney hitched herself out of the truck and came to see. They crowded around the vet.

"Now stand back," she ordered. "Mandy, you lift him out for me, let him have a sniff around, find out where he is."

Gently Mandy took Ricky out of the cage. He peered up at her, his funny little masked face poking this way and that, his tail twitching.

"Don't handle him too much," Lauren warned. "This is a wild animal, remember!"

So Joel and Courtney held back while Ricky got his bearings. He sniffed the air, looked this way and that.

"Up there!" Joel whispered suddenly, pointing into the high branches of the sea-grape trees. By this time Bee and Jerry, Grandpa and Grandma Hope had come out onto the porch to watch.

All heads turned in the direction of Joel's pointing finger. They heard a rustle among the broad, flat leaves, caught a flash of gray-brown fur, and a glimpse of a striped tail.

"Is it Rita?" Courtney murmured.

They followed the raccoon's progress through the trees. At last she emerged into clear view at the end of a branch, poised to leap.

"It is!" Mandy cried, holding Ricky up toward the tree-tops.

Then Rita jumped. She launched herself from the tree

toward the roof of the house, seeming to fly through the air. She landed and came scurrying down toward the porch, her eyes on Mandy and Ricky.

"See!" Mandy whispered, tiptoeing forward and reaching up so that the baby raccoon could scramble onto the porch roof. "Your mom came back for you!"

Then she stood back. They all watched the two animals meet up, turn for a moment to look down at their audience, then scamper off onto the high roof. They sat for a moment on the ridge, like two bandits on horseback, ready to ride off into the blazing sun.

Mandy grinned at Joel. "Don't worry, they'll be back!" she murmured.

Rita and Ricky flicked their tails, preparing to scamper away.

"Tonight, when it's time for supper!" she promised. In her own mind she felt sure that the raccoons on the roof were here to stay.

Read all the Animal Ark books!

by Ben M. Baglio

$3.99 US Each!